New York's FINEST

{TO THE DEATH}

KIKI SWINSON

NEW YORK TIMES BEST SELLING AUTHOR OF *WIFEY*

KS PUBLICATIONS
WWW.KIKISWINSON.NET

Publisher's address:
K.S. Publications
P.O. Box 68878
Virginia Beach, VA 23471

Website: www.kikiswinson.net
Email: KS.publications@yahoo.com
ISBN-13: 978-0986203749
ISBN-10: 0-986203742

First Edition: October 2018

Editors: J. Wooden & Letitia Carrington
Interior & Cover Design: Davida Baldwin
(OddBalldsgn.com)
Cover Photography: Davida Baldwin
(OBDPhotography.com)

ALSO IN STORES NOW:

What Now?

NAOMI

My life was always in an uproar. When I think back on my life as a flight attendant, all I keep reminding myself is how promising my future looked back then. I had it all. Money, foreign cars, real estate property, fur coats, you name it, I had it. But look at my situation now, I'm on the run once again with my family in tow. I know it's hard to believe, but my mother is tired of running from state to state. She's an older woman with a chill and laid-back personality. And the crazy part about this whole thing is that you'll never hear her complain about it. She loves my father and Reggie and me so much that she's willing to put up with anything to keep us all together. She's a goodhearted lady, and I only hope that I can be half of the person she is.

"Think Reggie is gonna get out of there?" My father asked me as we entered the corner restaurant. We purposely walked behind my mother so she wouldn't hear what we were saying.

"I don't know. Those cops were on his heels after he started firing his pistol at them." I replied after the door of the Tavern Café door closed behind us.

"Hey you guys, there's Damian." My mother pointed out as she pointed towards a table in the back of the diner but next to a window.

Seeing Damian sitting in the restaurant and out of harm's way gave me an overwhelming feeling. I rushed towards him and grabbed him into my arms immediately after he stood up. "Oh my God! I thought that I wasn't going to see again." I expressed to him between kisses.

"Where is Reggie?" He asked me.

Foxx spoke first. "Naomi said she saw him running towards the parking garage."

"Don't worry. I know my son. He'll be here with us any minute now." My mother said confidently.

Everyone looked at her and saw the optimism in her eyes. So, we knew that right now wasn't a good time to rain on her parade. I wanted Reggie to get away from those crackers, but Foxx, myself and Damian knew that the odds were stacked against him.

"Oh my! There he is." My mother blurted out loud as she pointed out of the window. My father Foxx, myself and Damian looked out of the window and saw Reggie running at the speed of lightning. "Where is he going?" My mother asked us. Before we could answer, she turned around and started towards the exit door of the Tavern. While my mother raced towards the front door of the café, Damian, myself and my father watched Reggie as he sprinted by. We did a double take when three police officers surfaced into our view. My heart collapsed into the pit of my stomach. My father and Damian stood there in complete shock. Before anyone of us could utter a word, one of the police officers shot Reggie twice in the back as he tried to elude them. Reggie immediately fell face down on the sidewalk across the street from the restaurant. I belted out a loud scream. Everyone in the café turned around and stared at me. Damian grabbed me and pulled me into his arms. He even tried to bury my face into his chest to prevent me from seeing Reggie lying on the ground, but I resisted him. "No, get off me!" I cried out. "They just killed my brother!" I shouted while I tried breaking away from Damian's hands. But he wouldn't let me go. That didn't stop me from trying to make a run for the door of the café. While I was trying to break free from Damian, my father instructed Damian not to let me come outside. "Please keep her in here." I heard him say.

"No, dad! I need to go and see if my brother is okay." I cried loud enough so that only he and Damian could hear me.

"Naomi, stop! You know you can't go out there. They will lock you up." He whispered in my ears as he held onto me. His grip on me got tighter.

I finally stopped resisting him and sat down in the booth next to me because he was right. If I'd run out of this café to see Reggie and confront the cops, they'd realize who I am, and I'd be locked up on sight. "What if he's dead?" I questioned Damian after he sat next to me. He was peering around me so he could get a first-hand look at what was going on outside.

"Let's just let your parents handle it." He said.

"Lord God! Please don't let my brother die." I continued to sob as I stared out of the window of the café.

It was pretty painful seeing my mother crying hysterically in my father's arms after he joined her outside. More than a dozen cops and plainclothes detectives showed up on the scene. Two of the cops that were standing near Reggie's body began to tape that area off with yellow tape. While the murder scene of my brother was being roped off, my mother and my dad were confronted by two plainclothes cops. My heart started beating in rapid speed. "What do you think they're saying to them?" I wondered aloud, still sobbing.

"I don't know. But let's hope that they don't find us sitting in this restaurant." Damian said to me.

I looked away from the window and turned my focus to Damian. I looked into his eyes and said, "What do you think we should do?"

"We're gonna have to slip out of here before this place gets flooded with cops. And if we're gonna do it, then we're gonna have to do it now." He informed me.

"But what about my parents?"

"They're gonna be fine. It's us that we're gonna have to worry about."

"Where are we gonna go?" I pressed the issue. I needed clarity. I needed him to give me more information than what he was giving me.

"Just wipe your face and come with me." He insisted and then he stood up from the seat in the booth. I followed him. As we walked out of the café, a few of the customers looked at us while the others continued to look at what was going on outside.

The moment the outdoor air hit me in the face, it became an instant reality that what was going on around us was real. I tried not to look at my parents for fear of breaking down, but it was impossible after I heard the loud cries of my mother. "Foxx, what are we going to do? They killed my baby boy!" I heard her sob. That instant I tried to pull away from Damian, but he wouldn't let me go. "Naomi, stop trying to fight me. I am not going to let you go. Now come on before the cops see us." Damian said to me, and then he gave me a swift tug.

I listened to Damian and followed his lead. We headed in the opposite direction of the cops and the apartment building we lived in. I swear it was hard leaving my family, but I knew it was in my best interest to do so. Damian and I walked half of mile until he figured out what we were going to do next.

"We're gonna check in that hotel up the block until we get back in touch with your parents." He told me.

"All right," I said while I continued to sob.

"Do you have your sunshades in your purse?"

"Yeah,"

"Put them on. I don't want the hotel employees to see you crying and think that I did something to hurt you."

"A'ight," I said, and then I pulled my Gucci sunshades out from my handbag and place them over my eyes.

It was Damian's idea to come to the Holiday Inn Express. It wasn't our usual five-star hotel, but I had no room to complain. We needed a safe haven, and at this point, that's all that mattered. "Go sit down and I'll get the room." He instructed me after we walked through the sliding doors.

"Welcome to Holiday Inn." A black woman said cheerfully. I took a quick glance at her and waved back at her. I couldn't act like I didn't hear her greet us. I mean, Damian and I were the only ones in the lobby.

"Hi there, I want to get a room." He said to the woman.

"Sure. Can I see your driver's license and a credit card?" She asked him.

"Yeah, here you go." He replied and slid before items across the counter.

I watched the woman grab Damian's I.D. and credit card and then she looked at it. "So, you're from New York, huh?" She questioned him and then she placed his I.D. down in front of her.

"No, I'm originally from New Jersey." I heard him lie to the desk clerk.

"I've been to New Jersey once." She bragged while she started tapping the keys on the computer keyboard.

"Only once?" Damian replied subtlety.

"Yep, only once. But I had a good time while I was there." She continued in a giddy like fashion.

"Good. I'm glad." He told her.

This chick was something else. She was definitely a talker. And she made it evident that she wanted to make conversation with him. I didn't say anything. I remained quiet while he handled his business. I figured that if I kept my mouth closed, then him getting a hotel room would run smoothly without any hiccups.

"Here are your key cards." She said as she slid the key cards across the counter towards him.

"Thank you." He said, and then he turned around towards me. "Ready?" He asked.

"Yes," I replied and stood up on my feet. It didn't take us long to take the elevator up to the second floor. Our room was only four doors away from the elevator, so we were inside the room in a matter of seconds. After Damian closed the door behind us, he locked it and tossed the key cards on the wooden stand next to the television. I, on the other hand, collapsed on the bedroom next to the window. I buried my face in one of the oversized pillows on the bed.

"Want something to drink?" I heard him ask me.

"No, I just wanna lay here by myself," I told him.

"Well, you do that, and I'm gonna go back outside to check on your parents." He replied and then I heard him leave the room. Deep down inside my heart was aching so I wanted to scream at the top of my lungs because I knew my brother was dead. I saw those fucking cowards shoot him right his fucking back. I swear, if I had an arsenal of firearms, I would've walked out of the café and took those motherfuckers out with every bullet I had. It wouldn't have mattered if they would've gotten a chance to take me out too. All of us would've been some dead motherfuckers when it was all said and done. *What am I going to do now?*

Looking Over My Shoulders

(DAMIAN)

The streets were crowded with cops, so I pulled my fitted ball cap down on my head and walked around with my head hung low. I didn't see Naomi's parents anywhere. I did notice that the cops hadn't removed Reggie's body from the spot where he fell. They did have a white sheet covering him, though. I went back into the Tavern Café so I could get a better view of what was happening around me.

"Will you be sitting at the bar area or will you prefer a booth?" A young, white waitress asked me.

"I'll rather sit at one of the booths in the back of the restaurant if I can."

"Yes, sure. Come on. I'll take you to the booth." She insisted.

"Thank you," I said.

"You're welcome." She replied as she led the way to the back of the restaurant. "Can I start you off with something to drink?" She continued after I sat down.

"Do you have sweet tea?"

"Yes, we do."

"Well, could I get a glass of that?"

"Would you like to have a couple of sliced lemons with it?"

"Yeah, sure," I told her.

"All right. I'll be right back." She said and then she walked away.

The moment she left my side, I turned my focus to the chaos going on outside the café. A small crowd of people congregated outside of the yellow tape the cops roped around the crime scene. They were talking amongst themselves while they observed all the activity going on around them. It was painful watching Reggie's lifeless body lying underneath the white sheet. My heart ached to know that he and I weren't going to run the streets anymore. Our business ties are done, and I have no one that I could trust to have my back. What am I going to do?

"Here's your sweet tea." The waitress said as she placed the glass down on the table in front of me.

"Thank you."

"No problem. Are you ready to order?" She wanted to know.

"No. I'm sorry. I haven't had a chance to look at the menu. So, I'm gonna stick with this for now. I'll let you know if I change my mind." I assured her.

"Okay, great. My name is Shelby. If you need anything, just let me know."

"I will. And thank you."

"You're welcomed."

Immediately after the waitress walked away from my table, I took a sip of the sweet tea and then I turned my attention back outside. I scanned the entire area from where I was sitting and still didn't see Naomi's parent anywhere. "Where the hell are you?" I mumbled to myself. "Damn, I sure hope the cops haven't taken them to their precinct." I continued to mumble.

While I was sitting in the booth and surveying the area, my cell phone started ringing. I looked at the caller ID and saw that it was Naomi calling me. I answered on the second ring. "What's baby?" I didn't hesitate to say.

"What's going on out there?" She wanted to know.

"Nothing really. There are more cops out there now than they were when we were out here."

"Where are my parents?"

"I don't know. I've been looking for them from the moment I came back out here."

"Where are you?"

"Inside the café."

"Have you tried calling Foxx?"

"Nah, I haven't."

"Well, I did, and his cell phone went straight to voicemail. I hope they are all right." Naomi seemed nervous.

"Don't worry about them. I'm gonna find them and bring them back to the room."

"Please do that. I don't know what I would do if I lost them."

"Naomi, I told you I got this, okay." I tried to reason with her.

She let out a long sigh. "Okay." She finally said.

She and I talked for a few more minutes and then I ended the call. Now I know she's dealing with the loss of her brother, but I can't deal with the whining and crying. I've got to stay level headed while I maneuver through these streets. Point Blank!

I sat here in this booth, watching everything going on around me for what seemed like an hour or more. The waitress stopped by my table a couple more times to see if I'd changed my mind about ordering something to eat. When I was expressing to her that I wasn't going to get anything to eat, I saw a man walking towards me in my peripheral vision. My heart skipped a beat when I turned my attention towards the person and realized that it was Foxx. I stood up and waited for him to approach me. "Man, I am so happy to see you," I said after he greeted me. By this time, the waitress had walked away.

"Where is Naomi?" Foxx wanted to know.

"We got a hotel room around the corner. So, I told her to lay low until I get back." I replied as we both took a seat.

"How is she taking everything?" Foxx's questions continued.

"All I can say is that she's pretty shaken up." I began to explain. "Where is mama?" I wanted to know.

"I walked her back to the apartment building. When I left the apartment, she was in our bedroom crying her eyes out."

I sighed heavily. "Why did the cops shoot him like that in broad daylight? They could've shot him in his legs. They didn't have to kill him." I pointed out.

"Yeah, I'm with you. We found out that he shot two police officers while he was trying to get away from."

"Did he kill 'em?"

"No,"

"So, why did they kill him?"

"I hate to say it, but you and I know that Reggie would've wanted to die rather than go to jail."

"Yeah, I know, but damn. It could've handled it a better way." I tried to reason with Foxx. Mama and Naomi are going to be scarred for life. Every time you think about Reggie, they're gonna think about this day and how the police g him down right in front of them."

"We're all gonna think about it," Foxx said, and then he turned his attention outside the glass window. "Look at that, shit! They still got my son laying out there in the street, with a white sheet covering him. They know they could've moved his body by now. But no, they wanted to torture my wife and me by treating him like a savage and leaving him out there for the whole world to see." Foxx continued.

"When you and your wife was out there, did they tell you how long they were going to keep him out there?"

"They said they were waiting for medical transport. But it's been over an hour. And it doesn't take that long to dispatch the city's coroner." Foxx explained. Do you know they asked me and my wife a ton of fucking questions about Reggie supposedly killing a married couple that lived in the building with us?"

"What did you say?"

"I told him we didn't know anything about it. And my wife told him that she didn't want to talk about it because she knew Reggie wouldn't anything like that. She basically shut the conversation down."

"What about Malika? Have they found the body?"

"Yeah, they found it."

"What did she say about that?"

"She told them that she didn't want to talk about that either."

"I know she's broken up inside," I mentioned. Mrs. Foxx was a beautiful lady. She had a good heart. She knew her son was a troublemaker. And a hothead. But to hear someone else talk about Reggie, she wasn't having it. She loved him no matter what he did. And in her eyes, he could do no wrong. So it was no surprise to me, that she refused to talk to the cops about him. "You know we need a new game plan, right?" I changed the subject.

Foxx turned his focus back on me. "Yeah, I know." He agreed.

"We need to get out of town. But in order to do that, we need money. And lots of it." I told Foxx.

"I've been thinking about that." He replied and then he fell silent.

"How long do you think it would take George's nephew to get rid of all the coke we got?" I initiated the question.

Foxx thought for a second and then he said, "According to George, I think they'll need at least 2 to 3 days."

"If they can do it in that time frame that would be great. The faster they make money, the quicker we can get out of here." I replied.

"Well, I'm gonna make a phone call to George right now," Foxx said, and then he pulled his cell phone from his front pants pocket. I watched Foxx as he dialed George's phone number and while he was waiting for George to answer, I glanced back out the window and watched the crowd as it doubled in numbers. Several news reporters were on site as well. And in the midst of all that, was Reggie's lifeless body, still covered in a white sheet. I looked at him, and wondered if he hadn't killed Malika or that married couple, would he still be alive? I swear, I wish I could turn back the hands of time. Regardless of what anyone says about him, he was a good guy at heart. And he'd give the shirt off his body. He was also a protector. He didn't have any problems with intimidating people, that caused his loved ones harm. That's just the way he was, and I will always have respect for him; even in his death.

While I thought back on all the good times Reggie and I had, I realized that Foxx had George on the phone. "Hey brother," Foxx started off saying, "me and my family ran into a situation, and we need your help." He continued.

I couldn't hear what George was saying, but I figured out some of the dialogue because of what Foxx was saying to him. "Okay, I'm gonna head over to your place now," Foxx said, and then he ended the call. When he looked back at me, he said, "He wants us to head over to his restaurant."

"How are we gonna get there?" I asked him.

"The garage entrance of the building is blocked off, so we're gonna have to take a cab," Foxx replied.

A'ight, well let's go." I told him, and then we got up and walked out of the diner.

Luckily for Foxx and I, we were able to jump in the very first cab we saw. After Foxx told the cab driver where we were going, he settled back in his seat and enjoyed the scenery. I can't say the same for the cab driver. "Hey, you guys what happened back there?" The white cab driver asked.

I looked over at Foxx, and he immediately knew that I wasn't opening my mouth, so he took the floor. "I think someone got shot," Foxx said.

"Who killed him?"

"One of the people in the crowd said the police shot him."

"In broad daylight?"

"So, it seems."

"What was he trying to rob a bank?"

"Not sure."

"That's probably what happened." He started off, "the cops in this city are some pretty laid-back guys. Their whole department has a good reputation around here. So, if they shot someone, it had to be because that guy probably shot at them first." The cab driver concluded. "So where are you guys from?" He changed the subject.

"Why you ask?" Foxx became serious as to why this man was asking him about where were we from.

"Because you have a northeastern accent. So, I figured that you weren't from around here."

"I'm from California," Foxx told him.

"Okay cool. What brings you to these parts?" The cab driver pressed the issue.

"We're just here visiting an old friend."

"Well, you came to the right place. We have a lot of nice restaurants in this part of town. We even have a nice comedy club here too. Make sure your friend take you to The Blue Crab. They have the best seafood gumbo in the world. Oh, and their crabcakes are good too. That's their signature dish."

"That sounds good. I'm gonna definitely check that place out."

"What kind of music do you guys listen to?"

"I like it all."

"Well if you're into the blues, there is this place called Dazzle, and you should check it out. They have live bands. And the food is awesome."

"I guess I'm going to check that place out too. I'm always down for good food and music." Foxx continued with his dialogue between him and the cab driver.

I got to be honest with you; the cab driver was getting on my fucking nerves. I wanted the dude to shut up, and I almost said it to him right after he asked Foxx where were we from. Foxx saw the frustration in my eyes and tapped me on the knee, giving me hand signals not to blow off some steam. I took instructions and remained quiet for the rest of the trip.

Fifteen minutes and thirty questions later, the cab driver finally got us to our destination. After Foxx paid him, we got out of the cab and headed inside George's restaurant. He only had one couple left in the restaurant. They were leaving out when Foxx and I were walking in. "Lock that door," George instructed us while he was standing behind the counter.

Foxx locked the door, and I walked over the counter and took a seat in one of the bar stools. "You guys want something to drink?" George offered.

"Nah, I'm good," I spoke first.

"Yeah, give me a bottle of water, if you have any," Foxx replied.

After George grabbed a bottle of spring water from utility glassed freezer behind the counter, he sat it down on the counter in front of Foxx. "So, what's going on?" George didn't hesitate to ask.

"Don't know if you saw it on the news, but the cops shot and killed Reggie a couple hours ago. Not only that, you know that my baby girl is wanted." Foxx started off saying.

"Ahhh, man. I remember the situation about your daughter. And now dealing with the loss of your son is fucked up. What happened?"

"He got into it with one of our neighbors. Words were exchanged, and he shot them." Foxx continued. But the information he was giving George, wasn't what really happened. I understood why Foxx gave George vague answers. Regardless of how close you are with someone, you never tell them the whole truth. Telling George that Reggie was dead, was all George needed to know.

"How many were there?"

"Two."

"Damn! That sucks! So, what are you guys going to do now?"

"We all need to get out of town. But we got all this coke that we need to get rid of. So, I thought if you can get your nephews together and let them know that we'll look out for them if they hurry up and get rid of the four kilos for us."

George wanted more details. "What are you talking?"

"Let 'em know that we'll give 'em 25 grand for each kilo if they can move it in three days," Foxx explained.

"Foxx that's not really a great deal. He can get 20 grand for kilo easy." George told him.

"I understand all of that. But we need to break even. Or we'll be hustling backwards." Foxx stressed to him.

"All right, I'll make a phone call and see what he says."

"Sounds good," Foxx said, and then we watched a George as he disappeared through the double doors that led to the kitchen.

While George was in the back making the phone call to his nephew Keith, Foxx and I sat on the stools and had a little small talk about our next move. "Think his nephew is gonna do it?" I asked.

"I guess we'll have to wait and see."

"You think three days is enough time to get rid of the dope?"

"It all depends. If there is a drought, we can probably get our money back in 48 hours."

"What are you guys going to do about Reggie?"

"We're gonna send his body back to New York, and bury him there."

"You know Naomi, and I aren't going to be able to come to his funeral."

"Yeah, my wife and I already talked about that. We'll take pictures and send them to you."

Before I could utter another word, George reappeared from the double doors. He was smiling as he walked towards us. "I take it that your nephew is going to help us out," Foxx spoke.

"Yes, he is. But, there is a catch,"

"What is it?" Foxx wanted to know.

"He said, he's going to need at least four days to pay you back."

Foxx looked at me, and I looked at him. I gave him a head nod, letting him know that four days was fine. So, he turned his focus back to George, and they shook on it. "Do you have the work now?" George asked.

"No. My wife has it. But I will get it back over here to you within the hour."

"Didn't I see you guys just get out of a cab?"

"Yes."

"Well, why don't I take you to your apartment and that way you could give me the drugs and I'll take them over to my nephew's spot."

"I've got one better," I interjected. "Why don't you take us back to the apartment, so that Foxx could get the drugs and we all ride over to your nephew's spot together. That way we can all come to an understanding about how this deal is going to be made." I continued.

"Let's do it." George agreed.

Foxx and I waited a few minutes so that George could gather his things. When he was done, he locked up the place, and then we left. On the way back to the apartment, George and Foxx exchanged dialogue about how he should handle Reggie's situation. I listen to him, but I didn't say a word. My mind was on Naomi. So, getting back to her was the next thing on my list.

I'm Losing My Mind

(NAOMI)

I dozed off and went to sleep for a couple of hours. I believe that I only woke up, because I sensed that Damian wasn't around. When I looked at the alarm clock near the lamp, I noticed that it was a little after 8 o'clock. Next, I picked up my cell phone and saw that Damian hadn't called, so this alarmed me. All sorts of things ran through my mind, like what if he was arrested? Or what if someone killed him? The thought of it gave me a sick feeling on my stomach. I felt pain in my heart too. I can't lose two people I love, in the same day. There's no way that that can happen.

Without giving it another thought, I dialed his number and waited for it to ring. Thank God he answered my call on the second ring. "Hey, babe you are right?" He spoke first.

"Yes, I'm fine. Where are you? You got me here worried about you."

"I'm good. I'm with Foxx and George. We're at his nephew spot handling some business. So as soon as we're done, I'm gonna come back to the room. Okay."

"Okay," I said. "Tell my father I love him."

"I sure will." He assured me, and then the line went dead.

I hadn't talked to my mother since we saw Reggie get killed. No matter how hard it was going to be to hurt her to talk about it, it was necessary to get her on the phone. After I dailed her number, it took the phone to ring five times before she answered it. And instead of saying hello, all I heard was her breathing, so I had to break the ice and say hello first. "Mom, how are you feeling?"

"I'm not too good darling." She replied softly. I could tell that she was crying, from the sniffling sounds she was making on the other end of the phone.

"Have you talked to the cops since earlier?" I wanted to know.

"No, I haven't."

"So, what are you going to do with his body?"

"I talked to your father, and we decided that we're gonna flying him back to New York."

"Is that where you guys are going to have his funeral?"

"Yes." She said and then she fell silent. I didn't know what else to say, so I remained quiet too. And then out of the blue, my mother hit me what a bombshell. "Why didn't you tell me that your brother killed Malika?"

"Mommy I don't think we should talk about that right now."

"And why not? Do you realize that she was pregnant with my grandchild?"

"Yes, mommy I know. But right now, isn't the time to talk about that."

"When will be a good time?" My mother asked sarcastically.

"I don't know. I do know that we shouldn't be discussing this over the phone."

"Well, who's going to call her family and tell them what happened?"

"You know I can't do it."

"I can't do it either. But somebody's got to call them."

"Let the cops do it. Isn't that their job?"

"Naomi, my head is spinning around in circles right now. I'm crying and pacing back and forth across these floors in this apartment. The neighbors in this building are whispering and coming up with their own theories. I can't get a spec of peace inside of my own place. Can you imagine how that feels?"

"Mom I'm going through the same things you're going through."

"So, what are we going to do about it?"

"I don't know. I'm sure Damian and dad are lining things up for us right now."

"I hope so." She said and then she exhaled. "I've gotta go."

"Okay. I'll talk to you later."

"All right."

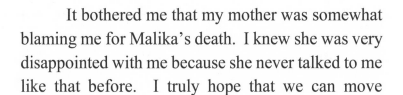

It bothered me that my mother was somewhat blaming me for Malika's death. I knew she was very disappointed with me because she never talked to me like that before. I truly hope that we can move beyond this so we could put our heads together and make the best decision from this day forward.

As bad as I wanted to call Damian back, I knew he was out taking care of business with my father, so that's what he needed to focus on. In addition to wanting to talk to Damian, I was starting to feel a little hungry too. Too afraid to go somewhere and get a bite to eat, I grabbed a couple of dollars from my handbag and went outside the room and grabbed me a Coca-Cola in a bottle and two bags of Bugles corn chips. On my way back to the room which was only twenty-steps away, I bumped into the desk clerk that checked Damian and me into our room. She smiled at me first and then she said, "I love Bugles."

I looked down at both of my bags, and then I look back at her. "I love them too," I told her.

"If you're really hungry, there's a diner on the corner. And they have chicken and dumplings that would knock your socks off."

"Thank you. I guess I'm gonna have to check them out."

"You won't be sorry." She continued as she walked by me.

I was so glad that she didn't stop and forced me to have a conversation with me. Maybe I let off the impression that I really didn't want to be bothered. If that was the case, then good for me.

As soon as I got back into the hotel room, I closed the door and locked it. I climbed on the bed, cracked open my first bag of chips, screwed off the bottle top of my soda and then I went to town. I figured this would hold me until Damian got back. Who knows maybe he'll bring me some takeout from one of these restaurants around here.

Kill or Be Killed

(DAMIAN)

When we first walked in George's nephew's trap house, we were met with two other guys, besides Keith. Now if something were to happen, the ratio between them and us would be uneven. Those odds would crush us before we knew it. Hopefully, nothing happens, because if it did, Fox and I would be some fighting ass niggas in this little ass trap house. We wouldn't have any room to get a fair fight. We'd be fucked for sure.

"Sorry to hear about your son," Keith said after he looked at Foxx.

"Thank you. I appreciate that." Foxx replied.

"So, my uncle says that you want to hurry up and get rid of what you got so you can leave town?"

"Yeah, that's exactly what we want to do."

"And you want it done in four days?"

"Yeah. George told me you said that you could make it happen."

"Yeah, I can do that. But I'm gonna need just a little bit more money."

"Look, I'm already taking a loss by giving you 25 per kilo," Foxx said. I could tell he was getting irritated really fast.

"I understand that. But I'm not the only one around here with good coke. I got competition out there. So, I'm gonna have to underprice them, just to get rid of this stuff in four days." Keith tried to explain.

I swear my blood pressure was rising. Listening to this dude, trying to play mind games with Foxx was really plucking my nerves. So, I have to say something. "Keith, check this out. Before Foxx and I walked in here, we had already had an understanding with George that we were going to give you each kilo for 25 grand. Now you wanna throw a bunch of bullshit in the mix and try to rob us for an extra five grand, I think that's fucked up. If the shoe was on the other foot, we wouldn't kick you if you were down."

"I'm sorry if you feel like I'm throwing bullshit in the mix. But, I'm a businessman. And businessmen make business decisions based on points that would make money. So, you see, paying you more money for coke that you're asking us to sell for you, doesn't make much sense to us. Now, if the tables were turned and we needed you, then we'd take you up on that offer. But being as though the ball is in our court, I'm gonna have to say 20 grand or no deal." Keith said, and then he fell silent. It seemed like everyone in the room was waiting for me to come back at Keith with a vengeance. And so was but Foxx, but he stopped me in my tracks.

"Listen, Keith; we're gonna do this deal with you for the 20k. But you have to promise us that you're gonna have our money back to us within four days. That means that you're going to have $80,000 for us by Sunday. Right?"

"Yeah gotcha," he agreed, and then he and Foxx shook hands.

Keith extended his hand towards me so I would shake it, but I just stood there and gritted on him. Did he really think that I wanted to shake his hands? Was he out of his damn mind? What I really wanted to do was spit on him. But I remained cool and held my composure. I figured it would be best that I let Foxx take the lead on this deal. He has more patience than I do.

"So. you don't want to shake my hands?" Keith directed his question at me.

"I only shake hands with men that aren't shiesty," I told him.

"So, you think I'm shiesty?" Keith pressed the issue.

"Yes, I do."

"Well, I'm sorry to hear that. I thought I was a shrewd businessman. Nothing more."

"Hey listen, you guys. It's not that serious." Foxx interjected. "The deal has been made. Let us all go home, get a good night's rest." Foxx continued.

"Speak for yourself," Keith said, and then he cracked a smile. "Me and my boys the grind and all night long. Don't we boys?"

"No doubt." One guy said.

"Damn right!" Another agreed.

"Sounds good. So, I guess we can get out of here." Foxx said to George and me.

"Yeah let's go," I replied, and then I walked out of the house. Foxx and George came outside about 30 seconds later. When we got back in Georgia's car, Foxx asked him to drop us back off to the diner near the apartment. On the way there,

George kept apologizing to Foxx and me about how things went down at his nephew's trap house. "I am so sorry you guys. I didn't mean for things to go down like you did. When I talked to Keith on the phone, he agreed to take 25 grand. So, to hear him say that he would only pay 20 grand, threw me for a loop."

"Well if it threw you for a loop, then why didn't you say something? Why didn't you remind him what he said over the phone?" I argued. George was pissing me off with that bullshit he was saying. He was acting like a bitch back at his nephew's spot.

"You heard what he said. He knew what we discussed when I talked to him on the phone. Remember he said he changed his mind." George pointed out

"Man, I'm not trying to hear that shit! You're bogus just like your nephew."

"Damian, don't worry about it. What's done is done. Let's just count this as a loss, get our money and start all over again when we get to where we're going." Foxx tried to compromise. He was working overtime to defuse this situation his friend put us in. But it's all good. We will bounce back after we leave this city.

George dropped Foxx and I off at the diner like we asked him to. Immediately after we got out of the car, I talked Foxx into walking to the hotel so he could see Naomi. After he agreed to do it, we headed in that direction.

When Foxx and I walked into the hotel room, Naomi was so excited to see Foxx. She hopped off the bed and jumped into his arm. "Daddy I am so happy to see you." She said.

"I'm happy to see you too." He told her. "Have you talked to your mother?"

"Yes, I have." Naomi started off saying as she backed away from Foxx and took a seat on the edge of the bed. "She didn't sound too happy when we were talking."

"She's really broken up behind Malika and your brother."

"Yeah, I know. Do you know that she blames me for Malika's murder?"

"She blames everyone, including me," Foxx told Naomi as he took a seat in the chair close to the door.

"She wants someone to call Malika's family and let them know what happened." Naomi pointed out.

"I told her to let the cops do it," Foxx said.

"Dad, I told her the same thing."

"Yeah, I think that would be the better idea," I interjected.

"Well, what did she say?" Foxx wanted to know.

"She didn't say anything. She just wanted to get off the phone. So, I let her."

"Just give her some time baby. She'll probably feel better tomorrow."

"I hope so because I don't like seeing her like this."

"I don't either," Foxx told Naomi.

"So, do we have a plan?" Naomi changed the subject.

"Well, Damian and I gave George's nephew all 4 kilos. And in return, he's going to give us $80,000 back. We're giving him four days to do that and as soon as we get the money, we're moving on." Foxx explained.

"You two gave them all four? Don't you think you're taking a big risk doing that?" Naomi seemed concerned.

"Under normal circumstances, I wouldn't have done it. But time isn't on our side, so I felt like

I made the best decision for the family." Foxx continued.

"You know if it was me, I wouldn't have done it," I interjected.

"I wouldn't have done either." Naomi agreed with me.

"What does George have to say about it?" Naomi asked, looking at both of us to see who was going to answer first.

"I'm gonna let Foxx answer that," I said, and then I turned my focus towards him.

Naomi looked at her dad and waited for him to speak. "Am I missing something?" she asked him.

"When we were at George's restaurant, he told us that his nephew would take the coke off our hands for one amount, but when we get to the spot, his nephew said something totally different. And that pissed Damian off." Foxx explained.

Naomi looked at me and then she looked back at Foxx. "That was kinda shady don't you think?" She commented while looking at Foxx.

"Yes, it was. But you know I'm a simple guy, and I don't do drama. Plus, we're working with a time restraint. So, we gotta do what we gotta do until we can do better."

"Are you sure he can get rid of 4 kilos in four days?" Naomi pressed the issue.

"If George said he could, then I believe him," Foxx replied.

"All right, well I guess that's settled," Naomi said.

I Need Some Understanding
(NAOMI)

fter we put the situation with George and his nephew, to rest, I brought a pressing issue to the forefront. "I don't think it'll be a good idea for me to go to Reggie's funeral. You know that as soon as the Feds find out that Reggie is dead, they're gonna put a lot of manpower to find out if I'm gonna attend it. And you know I can't have that." I explained.

"I've already thought about that," Foxx said.

"Do you think I'm being too paranoid?" I wanted to know. I needed my father's approval on any decision I make. He was old school. So, he knew what will be best for me.

"You're not being paranoid. I'm glad you're thinking ahead. You always gotta be two steps ahead of the enemy." He told me.

"Mom said she'll take pictures and send them to me."

"That doesn't surprise me. You know she loves you and your brother."

"Yes, daddy I know."

"Do you think she'll ever get over seeing Reggie getting murdered?" Damian asked Foxx.

"I don't think so. I think she's gonna carry that burden on her heart until the day she dies." Foxx replied.

"She sounded like she was out of it when I talked to her over an hour ago," I told them.

Right when Foxx was about to speak someone knocked on the hotel room door. It felt like I was about to have a panic attack. All three of us became radio silent. I swear I didn't know what to do. Foxx and Damian acted like they didn't know what to do either. Whoever was on the other side of the door knocked a total of five times. "Who do you think it is?" I whispered to Damian.

"I don't know." He replied.

"Maybe it's housekeeping," Foxx suggested. His words were barely audible.

"If it was housekeeping, they would've identified themselves by now," I said.

While we were sitting there trying to debate whether or not we should answer the door, a voice on the other side said, "Hey you guys, it's Patra from the front desk. I've got some pizza coupons for you if you want them."

Relieved that it was the lady that checked us in this room, but then that relief turned into aggravation. "Why the fuck does she want to bother us with some damn pizza coupons? Did you ask for them?" I asked Damian.

"No. I didn't. I haven't seen her since we checked into the hotel." He told me.

"Just get the coupons and send her on her way," Foxx said.

Damian stood up and walked to the door. When he opened it, this chick was smiling from ear to ear. I couldn't see Damian's face because he was facing her. "I was talking to your wife earlier when she was at the vending machine. I was telling her about a restaurant that we had down the street. I thought I had some coupons for that restaurant, but I didn't. I did find these pizza coupons though. It's a buy one get one free deal." She explained.

Damian took the coupons from her and thanked her.

"You're welcome." She said and then she walked away from the door.

After Damian closed the door, he locked it and then he turned around and faced Foxx and me. "She's weird." He commented.

"Tell me about it," I replied sarcastically.

"Sounds like you guys have a new friend." Foxx joked. The joke was corny, but I knew why he said it. He'd do anything to keep me and my mother in good spirits. That's just the kind of man he was. I swear, I wouldn't know what to do if I didn't have that man in my life. He is definitely our rock.

Two hours passed and neither one of us realized it until my mother called Foxx to see where he was and when he was coming back to the apartment. "I'll be home in the next 30 minutes." He told her. She didn't put up any fuss. She told him, okay, and then their call ended. "Do you guys know how long you're gonna be in this hotel?" Foxx asked Damian and me.

"At least until we get the money from that nigga Keith," Damian replied.

"I don't think it's safe. What if you guy's faces get plastered all over on TV on an episode of America's Most Wanted? That desk clerk would probably be the first one to rat you two out."

"Where would we go?" I asked him because he was right. Homegirl was definitely trying her best to get all friendly with us. I'm too old to be making new friends, but I don't think she noticed.

"Come and stay at the apartment with your mother and I. You and Damian could stay in the guest room. It'll be just like old times. That way we can all look after each other."

"Yeah Naomi, I think he's right." Damian agreed.

"When do you think we should come?"

"Early in the morning. Before the sun comes up." Come through the garage entrance."

I looked at Damian. "Are you okay with that?" I asked him.

"Yeah, I'm good with that arrangement."

"So, then I' guess it's settled. But don't tell mama, daddy. Let it be a surprise." I instructed him.

"I won't sweetheart!"

Before Foxx got up and said goodbye to us, he made Damian, and I promise that we weren't going to make any decisions for this family unless he was involved. After we promised him that we would do just that, he kissed me on my forehead and told me that he loved me. My heart always flutters when my dad tells me he loves me. No one in the world can replace that man. And I mean no one.

Selling Your Soul
(DAMIAN)

Immediately after I let Foxx out of the room and locked the door, I went back and laid down on the bed next to Naomi and told her how much I loved her. "You don't need to tell me you love me. You show me every day that you do." She told me.

"I know that. But doesn't it feel good to hear it every now and again?" I pointed out.

"Yeah, it does" she replied, giving me the full attention.

"Why don't you tell me how you're feeling?" I changed the subject.

"I'm experiencing all sorts of feelings. I can't tell you if I'm coming or going." She told me.

"Were you serious when you said that you weren't going to Reggie's funeral?"

"Yeah, I'll be setting myself up if I showed up. You know the church would be crawling with cops."

"I sure wished that he hadn't started shooting at those cops."

"I keep saying that myself. He probably would've gotten away if he hadn't gone in the parking garage."

"I believe that too."

Naomi buried her face in her hands and then she looked back up. Instead of looking at me, she started watching the television. That's when I noticed how watery her eyes had become. After a few tears rolled down her cheeks, I sat up on the bed and started rubbing her back. "It's gonna be all right," I assured her.

"But what if it doesn't? What if everything we've worked so hard for, starts to fall down around us? Do you know how much I missed working? I lived for flying all over the country. I had some terrific friends that worked with at me at the airlines too. We used to do everything together. We ate at nice restaurants. We shopped anywhere we wanted. I swear, those were some of the best times in my life. But look at me now, I'm running around from state to state trying to keep the DEA off my ass, and losing my brother in the process. My life is fucked up now." She expressed.

My heart went out to Naomi for all the pain she had bottled up inside of her. She was a good girl. But she has to remember that she chose this life. She was the middleman for Reggie's drug cartel contacts. She opened that door, not me nor Reggie. I wished things were different, but it's too late. Once you get in the life, that's it.

I tried to console her as much as I could. In the end, she cried herself to sleep, and I laid there and watched her. She looked peaceful, but that was at the surface. Deep down inside she was dealing with a lot. When she expressed to me how she missed her job, her friends, traveling all over the country and eating at nice restaurants, I knew what that really meant. Naomi was used to the good life. Before me, she dated some very wealthy drug dealers, and there was nothing they wouldn't give her. A woman like her isn't used to the struggle. Even back when she and Reggie were kids. Foxx took care of them. He was dealing drugs very heavy back in the days, so they walked around like little rich kids. So, you see, this right here isn't apart of her element. I wished I could do something to take her mind off our current reality, but I can't. The only thing left for us to do is, work with the cards we were dealt. It's simple as that.

Me, being the type of guy, I am, I don't wear my heart on my sleeves. I'm one of those hardcore ass dudes that had little or no patience. And sometimes that wasn't a good thing, especially when there's a woman in the mix. My only hope is that Foxx and I get our money and get the hell out of this city. Nothing else will make me happier.

I think I only had about three hours of sleep, before Naomi and I got up and gathered our things to head back over to the apartment building we shared together. But instead of going back into our apartment, we were going to lay low in her parents' place. I hope no one recognizes us while in route to Foxx's spot.

"Ready to get out of this joint?" I asked her.

"Yes, I am." She replied and then she grabbed her things and followed me out the door.

I called Foxx to let him know that Naomi and I were on our way to the apartment. When I told him that we'd be there in the next 5 to 7 minutes, he told me that he would be looking out for us and after he told us to be careful we ended the call. Now as we were walking by the corner diner, Naomi sparked up a conversation about Reggie killing Malika. "How did you feel when you found out that Reggie killed Malika?" Her questions started off.

"I was shocked for one. I mean, I knew he was getting tired of her. But I never thought that it would get to that point where he'd kill her."

"You do know that it was an accident, right?"

"Yeah, Foxx told me."

"How do you feel about my brother now after knowing what he did?"

"I really don't feel any differently about him. Reggie was like a brother to me. And through the years of us growing up together, he has done a lot of stupid shit, but it never got to the point where I didn't like him or cared less for him. We were like a ride or die." I began to explain. "But why did you ask? Am I doing something that's making you think that I feel differently about him?"

"No. I was just curious."

"Well, how do you feel?" I turned the question back on her.

"I love my brother to death. But sometimes he used to take stuff overboard. It's like he didn't care about crossing boundaries. I know I've bailed him out of a dozen situations. I even persuaded a drug lord from Panama from killing him. That night was crazy. I will never forget it."

"Reggie was definitely a hothead. Sorry, he had to go out of here the way he did."

"Me too." She said and then she fell silent. "I guess all we can do now is pray that he's in a better place." She continued.

"Let's hope so."

Family Reunion
(NAOMI)

D amian and I jumped through hoops to get through the garage undetected. And when we got near the door of the garage, Damian called Foxx so we could get in the building. Now we could've used our security card, but every entry into the building is computerized. So, if we'd use it, then it would be documented in their alarm system.

When my father opened the door to the garage, he greeted me with the biggest smile ever. "Come on in here, baby girl." He said and took all my bags out of my hands.

After I walked by my dad, I headed straight down the hallway to his apartment. I heard him and Damian engaging in small talk while they followed me. "Did you guys get some rest?" My dad asked Damian.

"She slept the whole night. I think I only got two to three hours' worth."

"Sounds like you got more sleep than me." I heard Foxx say.

Before Damian could comment I had already entered the apartment. As soon as I got within 5 feet of my mother's bedroom, her door opened. "Hey, mama," I spoke first.

She smiled and started walking towards me. "Hi, sweetheart. What are you doing here?"

"Dad said that we all needed to be together," I told her as I embraced her. It felt good to have her arms wrapped around me. It also felt good to have her in my arms as well. I love my mama. And I know she loves me.

"Where is he?" She asked.

"I'm right here woman." He said as soon as he crossed the entryway of the front door. Damian came in behind him.

"Hey, Mrs. Foxx," Damian said as he placed his things on the coffee table in the living room. He walked over and gave her a hug a few seconds later.

"What are y'all doing up so early?" My mom asked us.

"It's better to do things while everyone around you was still asleep," Damian answered.

"Are you guys hungry?" My mother wanted to know.

"I know I am," I spoke first.

"Yeah, I could use some food on my stomach too." Damian chimed in.

"Well then, it's settled. Go put your things in I guest bedroom and then go and wash your hands."

"Will do," Damian spoke first, and then he followed me to the guest bedroom.

"Your mother is really happy that you're here with her." Damian pointed out after he closed the bedroom door.

"I know. When she hugged me, she acted like she didn't want to let me go."

"That's probably because she doesn't."

"You might be right," I said, and then I changed the subject. "Think anyone in the building saw us?"

"Stop being so paranoid. Everyone in the building is probably still asleep."

"Trust me; someone is always watching. I learned that from working for the airlines. So, we're gonna have to stay incognito until we leave this place for good." I said while hanging up the few items of clothes I had in the walk-in closet.

"Sounds good to me." He replied while he was putting his clothes away in the dresser drawers.

"I wonder if mom has plans to go in Reggie's apartment to collect all of his things."

"Why don't you ask her?"

"What if she hasn't? I don't wanna dig up wounds and make her upset."

"Why don't you just ask Foxx? If she thought about it, then he would know."

"You definitely have a point there."

"That's what I'm here for baby." He said, and then he walked over to where I was and pulled me into his arms. "I don't know what I would do without you." He continued, as he looked me directly in the eyes.

"I sometimes say the same thing," I told him, and I meant every word. Damian was my guardian angel now. I know Reggie is looking down on us and is very pleased to see how he has stepped up to the plate. All Damian needs to do now is, get us out of this place and into another safe haven before the cops find out where we are. "Let's go freshen up so we can get something to eat," I added, and then I kissed him on the lips.

My mom whipped up a plateful of turkey bacon, scrambled eggs with cheese, and she completed it with fried potatoes and onions. I swear, it felt like old times when she would invite Reggie and me over to her house on Sunday for breakfast. When I was in town, I was always there. It sucks that Reggie isn't here with us. If he was here, he would be the life of the party. "Mama, you put your foot in these potatoes," I commented. My mother loved when we complimented her on how great she can cook.

"I'm glad you like it." She replied. For the first time since the death of my brother, I got to see my mother smile again. This meant so much to me. I just hope that we can keep her smiling.

After breakfast was over, Damian and my father retreated to the living room area of the apartment while my mother and I cleaned up around the kitchen. Ten minutes into cleaning, we all heard a knock on the front door. Everyone in the apartment fell silent, while my heart dropped into the pit of my stomach. "Are you expecting someone?" I whispered to my mother.

"No." She whispered back.

A couple of seconds later, Foxx and Damian treaded lightly back into the kitchen. "Do you have any idea who that could be?" My dad asked my mom.

"No. I have no clue who that could be." She continued to whisper.

"Everybody stay here. I'm gonna see who that is." My dad said, and then he headed towards the front door.

My mother, myself and Damian stood quietly in the kitchen, so my father could find out who was knocking at their door. "Who is it?" I heard him say.

"Detective Franco, sir." I heard a man say.

I instantly looked at Damian, and then I looked at my mother as fear consumed me. "Oh my God! They know that Damian and I are here." I panicked.

"Calm down. Foxx will handle it." Damian murmured, making sure that only me and my mother could hear him.

"What do you need?" My father yelled through the door.

"I just need to ask you a few questions." The cop pressured him.

"I'm listening." He told the guy.

"Sir, if you open the door, we will only take up a few minutes of your time." The cop pressed the issue.

My father must've realized that the cop wasn't going anywhere, so he finally decided to open the door. "What can I help you with?" He continued after he opened the door.

"My name is Detective Franco, and this is my partner Detective Myers, and we're out here investigating the triple homicide that happened yesterday."

"Well, if you're investigating those homicides, then why are you standing here talking to me?" My father said sarcastically.

"Well, sir we're here because from what we were told, the murders were done by your son's hands." The same cop said.

"Did my son tell you that?"

"No, sir. He's deceased."

"Well, that's too damn bad! Now if you don't mind, I've got to get back to my breakfast before it gets cold."

"Can I leave you with my card?"

"No, you may not," Foxx said, and then I heard him shut the front door. I swear, I couldn't believe it. My father shut those assholes down. Not

here? I'm sure he has some things in there that you guys would want to take with you."

"Yeah, I'm gonna go up there and check things out."

"Good. Because you don't want the apartment manager taking things out of there that didn't belong to 'em."

"Trust me, I thought about that too." He said, and then he turned the question around to me. "What about you? Do you and Naomi have anything in your apartment that you want to get out?"

"I can't think of anything. Not right now. She may have something there that she wants."

"Have what?" Naomi interjected as she entered the living room.

"He was asking me if we had some stuff in our apartment that we left and wanted to get out of there," I told her.

"Yes, I have a lot of things in there that I want to get out."

"Like what?" I asked her.

"Like, my curling iron. My bedroom shoes. My gold hoop earrings. And I also left my Beats earplugs on the nightstand in the bedroom."

"Are you sure you didn't leave the refrigerator too." I joked.

"No smart ass! But I did leave a couple of packs of yogurt and there."

"Are you serious?" I questioned her because she can get it pretty sarcastic sometimes.

"I'm just kidding silly." She clowned around as she plopped down on the sofa next to Foxx. Foxx and I both chuckled at her humor.

"You guys need me to do anything before I get into the shower?" Foxx's wife asked us after she appeared before us.

"No mama, I'm good," Naomi spoke first.

"No honey, I'm fine. Thanks for asking though." Foxx replied.

I gave her the old-fashioned head nod. She knew that meant that I was fine too.

"Well let me know if you guys need anything." She offered and then she disappeared down the hallway.

When we heard her bedroom door close, Naomi was the first one to say something. "She was so happy before those cops knocked on the door," Naomi mentioned.

"Yeah, I noticed that." I chimed in.

"Don't worry about her. Your mother is a very strong woman." Foxx said to Naomi.

"I hope so. I mean, she's already dealing with the fact that she's gotta bury Reggie. And then those fucking cops show up talking about him killing three other people." Naomi explained.

"Baby girl, you don't have to get all worked up. Your mother is going to be fine. Mark my words." Foxx tried assuring Naomi.

"I know. I know. I'm just so sick of this place. If we could leave right now, I would be packing my things." Naomi expressed.

"Me and you both." I agreed with her because she was right. We've only been in town for only a couple of days, and in those few days, three people have been murdered. We had to leave our apartment. Stay in a hotel so we won't be on the cop's radar. And now, we're taking a huge hit on four kilos of coke that we bought a couple days ago. What kind of shit is that? Hopefully, things will come together in the end. But if it doesn't, then we're up shits creek without a paddle.

Thirty Minutes Later
(NAOMI)

Damian insisted that if my dad was going to Reggie's apartment, then he needed to go now while it's still early. As much as Damian wanted to accompany him, I ended up talking him out of it. "You don't need to go with him. What if you guys run into the same cops that were here earlier?" I pointed out.

"Yeah, Damian she's right." My dad agreed with me.

"I'll tell you what, why don't you let me go alone this time. But while I'm away you two could listen to every step I make from the time I walk in

Reggie's apartment and until I come back here? He suggested.

"I think that's a good plan," I said aloud.

Damian hesitated for a few seconds, and then he finally agreed.

"Be careful dad," I said as he left the apartment. Immediately after he got off the elevator, he called us so we could hear everything. "I just got off the elevator." He told us.

"Well we're gonna put you on mute, so no one on your end hears us," I said.

"Good thinking." He complimented me. That's just like my dad; he wasn't stingy with compliments. "I'm putting you on mute right now." He continued.

Damian and I sat on the sofa of my parents living room and listened intently as Foxx headed to Reggie and Malika's apartment. It felt like my heart wanted to jump out of my chest, while I thought about all the crazy beings that could happen while he's traveling alone on this mission. I hoped and prayed that he'd be okay on his own.

"There's yellow tape crisscrossed over the front door to prevent anyone from going inside the apartment. What do you think I should do?" He wanted to know, as he whispered through the phone and then he acknowledged that he took us off mute.

"Tear the tape down and go inside," I answered him.

"All right." He replied. And then he said, "I'm putting you guys back on mute."

Neither myself nor Damian replied. We just sat there and waited for my father to say something else.

"I see a lot of black shock and dust on the walls, so I'm assuming the forensics people dusted for fingerprints. I even see a few things in the living room turned over, like Malika and Reggie had a big fight." My father continued. From there Damian and I heard footsteps. "I'm in their bedroom now." He whispered. "I don't see anything out of place. It looks like nothing happened in here." He spoke further. A few seconds after that, we heard more footsteps. "Excuse me, is anyone in here?" Damian and I heard another voice. It was the voice of a man, and it startled us. I wanted to cover my mouth to prevent me from breathing loud so that the person in the room with my father wouldn't hear me on the other end of my father's phone. But then it dawned on me that my father had me on mute, so he wouldn't hear me anyway. It's funny how your mind plays tricks on you.

"Who do you think that could be?" Damian whispered.

"I don't know," I replied.

"Who are you looking for?" I heard my father say.

"I wasn't looking for anyone because this apartment is supposed to be empty that's why the yellow tape was on the front door." The answered.

Once again I heard footsteps. "You work here in the building, right?" I heard my father say.

"Yes. I'm apart of security here. The homicide detectives don't want anyone in here until their investigation is final." The guy explained.

"Sorry about that. But this is my son's apartment, and I only came in here so that I could get his things." I heard my dad tell the guy.

"How did you get in here?"

"He gave me a spare key when he and his girlfriend first move in here."

"Okay, well I'm gonna let you hold onto that. But I'm gonna have to ask you to leave. Just until they say differently."

"What can I at least get a few of his things?"

"No, I'm sorry, but I can't let that happen."

"All right. I'll leave." My father gave in.

"Thank you, sir. I appreciate you cooperating. And not giving me a hard time."

"I understand, you're just doing your job." My dad said as he sucked up to the guy. What he really wanted to do was to tell the guy to go and fuck off. Talk about using reverse psychology. He had that skill on lock.

"Look, I'll tell you what," the guy started off, "if your son got any pictures or other personal stuff like his ID, then I'll let you get. The big stuff like the TV and furniture is gonna have to stay here." The guy concluded.

"I appreciate that….." I heard my dad say and then he fell silent.

"It's Doug. My name is Doug. I work in the security office." The guy said.

"Thank you, Doug. You're a stand-up guy."

"I hope you don't mind, but I'm gonna have to stay here until you leave."

"Oh no. I don't have a problem with that." My father told him. "Just let me go into the bedroom and see if he has those things laying around." My father continued, and then I heard footsteps. As a matter of fact, Damian and I heard a ton of footsteps. I sounded like my dad was walking in every part of

Reggie's apartment. So for the next minute and a half, there was footsteps, opening, and closing doors and then we heard a few objects being shifted. "I didn't find any pictures lying around, and I didn't see his wallet or other personal things. But I did find his girlfriend's purse, so I'm gonna take that and give it to her family when they come here tomorrow." I heard my dad say.

"Okay, great." The guy said then Damian, and I heard more footsteps.

Seconds later, we heard the door closed. We figured that was either my dad or the security guy closing the front door to Reggie's apartment. "Thanks, again man." My dad said.

"No problem." The guy replied.

For about twenty seconds, there was complete silence. But then, we heard the elevator door chimed, and then it sounded like it opened. Without notice, his cell phone died. We completely lost his call. Damian and I both looked at the phone, and then we looked at each other. "What do you think happened?" I asked Damian.

"He lost the signal after the elevator door closed."

"I think you're right." I agree with him, but at the same time hoping that what he said was true.

A couple of seconds later, the front door opened. I let out a sigh of relief when my father appeared from the other side of the door, carrying Malika's oversized Gucci bag in his hand. I got up from the chair and walked towards him. Damian's stayed seated on the couch. "I was so scared for you when I heard that man asked who was in the apartment," I said.

"Yeah, that caught me off guard." My dad admitted.

"I thought it was the cops," Damian said.

"Me too," I added. "Thank God that he was nice about it." I continued.

"He may have been nice in the end, but you should've seen his face when he first saw me. He was very intimidating." My dad continued explaining.

"What are y'all in here talking about?" My mother asked as she reentered the living room. "And why do you have Malika's purse in your hand?" She directed the question to my father.

"I got it from Reggie Malika's apartment."

"So you went there after all?" My mother added and took a seat on the opposite end of the sofa.

"Yeah, I did. And while I was in there, when is the security guys from the building caught me in there and asked me to leave." My dad told her.

"Did you tell him that that was your son's apartment?" My mother wanted to know.

"Yeah, I told him that."

"And what did he say?" My mother pressed the issue.

"He told me that no one is supposed to be in there because it was a crime scene and that the homicide investigators have banned anyone from going in there until they say differently."

"Oh really?" My mother continued.

"Yes darling, really."

"So, what made you take Malika's purse out of the apartment?" She wanted to know.

"I figured that it was best to get his so we can give it to her family when we see them."

"Okay," my mother said, but in her mind, she could really care less. She had a son that's deceased. And he wasn't coming back, so I took the incident involving the security guard was of no interest to her. I swear, I hope my mother bounce back after this ordeal.

"Let's see what's in her purse," I said.

"Here you go. Take it." My father said with no problems and handed me Malika's purse.

I sat back down on the sofa and dumped all the contents of Malika's purse on to the coffee table. To the naked eye, it appears that she had the normal things that a woman will have in their purse. A tube of lipstick. A container of lip gloss. Eyelashes. A Gucci wallet. You name it; it was in there. So, as I began to put her things back into her purse, I thumbed across a little book. And when I turned it over and looked at the cover, it was labeled as a journal. So being the nosy person that I am, I opened it. The first date she started writing in was, July 11th, 2017., which was one year and five months ago. Some of the passages talked about how she called my brother cheating and that she was tired of him screwing around on her. Other passages in there she talked about how he took her out to dinner and how they made love later that night. She even talked about how she stole thousands of dollars from him he didn't know it. She got a crack out of that. I guess she felt like her actions were justifiable because of the many times he cheated on her. From the looks of her journal, it looks like Reggie cheated on her at least a couple of times a month. I swear my heart went out to her when I read that. I guess what they say was true; my brother was definitely a ladies' man.

Out of all the passages in her journal, one particular one stuck out to me. I read it to myself first, but when what I said, registered in my mind, I had to read it out loud to my family. "Mama, you're not going to believe this," I warned her.

"What is it?" She wanted to know.

By this time, I had gotten everyone's attention. "It's dated February 17th, 2018. And it says, *I just found out that I was pregnant. But I'm scared because I don't know if it's Reggie's baby or not. I don't know what I am going to do. Should I have an abortion? Or should I keep it? What if my baby is Ryan's baby? Reggie would kill me if he found out that I even crept with Ryan. I knew I should've made him use a condom. Damn! I need help with this. But who could I tell? My mother would be so disappointed in me that I would slip up and do something like this. It's bad enough that she doesn't like street guys. And I can't tell my best friend. She would love to smear this news all in Reggie's face. She hates the ground she walks on. Maybe I just need to pay for the abortion. At least then, I'll be able to start over fresh and not make this mistake again. God, please send me a sign.*"

After I read Malika's journal entry, I looked around the room at everyone's facial expression. He looked like Damian wasn't shocked at all. But I can't say the same about my parents. "Oh my God! So, she's saying that that baby she was carrying may not have been my grandchild?" My mother questioned me.

"That's what it seems like," I replied.

"Oh goodness! I used to think so highly of her. What has gotten into her head?" My mother's questions continued.

"Maybe it was because Reggie kept cheating on her with different women."

"I don't care how many women a man cheats with, as a woman you should never stoop so low. Your cheated on me once and did I go out and do it? No!"

"Honey, did you have to tell them I cheated on you?" My dad said.

"Come on now dad; this is not the first time she told me this story." I tried to level the playing ground.

"Listen, Naomi, always remember that you can't stop a man from doing what he wants to do. But you can remove yourself from that toxic environment. So, what I am saying here is that I don't feel sorry for Malika. She did that mess to herself. Maybe Reggie already knew this, and that's why he killed her?"

"No, mama. He didn't know."

"How do you know that he didn't know?"

"Because he would've told me," I said with assurance.

"Yeah, he would've told me too. So, I don't think he knew." Damian chimed in.

"I guess, it doesn't matter anyway you look at it, huh? She's dead and can't no one bring them back." My mother concluded.

Three Days After Reggie's Murder

(DAMIAN)

After three days, Mr. and Mrs. Foxx finally got the okay, to see Reggie's body. They even filled out the paperwork to have his body shipped back to New York. The county morgues office assured them that Reggie's body would be delivered in the next 5 to 6 days, so that's what they agreed upon.

On their way back, they called us and wanted to know if we wanted something to eat while they were out. Naomi and I agreed on deli subs from Subway, so that's what they brought us back.

We greeted them with smiles when they entered into the apartment. And as they made their way into the kitchen, Naomi and I got up and followed. "I can't wait to sink my teeth in that sub," I said as I rubbed both of my hands together.

I took a seat at the bar area of the kitchen and waited for my sub to be passed to me. When Naomi finally gave it to me, she handed me several napkins too. "Eat up." She told me.

"I will. Don't you worry." I told her.

Foxx took a seat on the bar stool next to me. From the looks of it, he ordered himself a roast beef sub with a little extra of everything on it. I'm talking extra meat, lettuce, mayo, cheese, onion, tomatoes, salt, pepper, vinegar. You name it; it was on his sub.

"Foxx, you sure you can handle that?" I joked.

"Why don't you just sit there and watch me." He smiled and then he took his first bite.

"Daddy, don't kill yourself over there," Naomi said with amusement.

"I'm fine baby girl. Now if you hear me coughing over then, then come and check on me. Other than that, just leave me be." He said then he took another bite.

"Foxx, why don't you tell them what the police said to us after we walked out of the county's morgue's office today." Mrs. Foxx interjected.

"You guys saw the cops again?" Naomi asked. She acted like she couldn't believe it.

"Yeah, we did," Foxx answered her.

"What did they say?" Naomi pressed the issue.

"They wanted to know if we had changed our mind and wanted to talk to them."

"What did you say?" Naomi wouldn't let up.

"Your mother and I both told them to leave us alone. We even told them that we're hiring an attorney if they harassed us again."

"What do they have to say then?" I joined the conversation.

"They went on a rant about how Reggie killed innocent people. And for the sake of their parents, we should want to help them. You know, give their families closure."

"That's bullshit daddy! They just want you to incriminate your own child." Naomi blurted out.

"We already know that baby girl." Foxx agreed with Naomi.

"Did they say anything about us?" I wanted to know. So far none of the cops mentioned me or

Naomi, which is a good thing. But we still need to know if our name has crossed their radar.

"No. No one has mentioned you or Naomi."

"They know that Reggie was a wanted man back in New York."

"Really!?" Naomi said. She looked spooked. And I can tell that her life flashed before her eyes.

"What did they say about that?" I asked Foxx.

"They just said that when they put his name in the system, his paperwork came back that he was a wanted man," Foxx explained.

"And he didn't say anything about me or Naomi?" I pressured Foxx to give me more information.

"No, they didn't. And believe me you, I was more shocked than you are now." Foxx reassured me.

"Did they say anything else?" Naomi asked.

"Nope. That was it." Foxx replied.

"You know we're gonna have to be extra careful. Because for all we know, they could be watching this building, waiting to see if Naomi and I pop up." I said to everyone in the kitchen.

"They may have already been in our apartment, and that's why they didn't ask about us." Naomi tried to reason.

"That could be true." I agreed with her.

"Whether they been there or not, we're gonna have to stay off the radar. We have no room for any mess-ups. Is that understood?" Foxx announced.

Every one of us agreed. While we were putting our heads together about what would be the best time to get out of here for good, we heard another set of knocks at the front door. We all looked at each other with facial expressions of fear. Naomi and her mother facial expressions were more of a look of terror. After the person at the front door knocked a total of four times, the knocks stopped. It looked like we all holding our breaths and hoping at the same time that whoever it was, had figured out that we weren't here and left.

"Think they're gone?" Mrs. Foxx asked.

"Shhhh…." Foxx said, and as soon as he said it, the knocking started again. This time they knocked five times, and from the looks of it, they weren't going to stop. This infuriated Foxx so much that he got out of his seat and stormed to the front door. Instead of asking who it was, he unlocked the door handle and swung open the door. "What do you want?" I heard him roar. He was pissed.

"How you doing Mr. Foxx. Remember me, Doug from the security office?" I heard the guy say.

"Yes, I remember. I'm sorry about that. I thought you were somebody else." Foxx replied.

"I'm sorry too. I came up here to let you know that we just got clearance from the detectives to let you go back into your son's apartment at your leisure."

"When did they give you the green light?" I heard Foxx ask him.

"Maybe five, ten minutes ago." He answered Foxx.

"It was actually eight minutes ago." Everyone in the kitchen heard an unfamiliar voice correct the security.

"And you are?" Foxx asked the new guy.

Before the new guy told Foxx who he was, the security, said, "I guess that's my cue. Mr. Foxx, if you need anything, please let the concierge manager know."

"I will. Thank you."

"No problem sir."

Once again everyone in the kitchen looked at each other. I looked at Naomi and Naomi looked at her mother. And then Naomi and her mother both looked at me. "Who is that?" Naomi whispered to me.

Without saying a word, Mrs. Foxx walked out of the kitchen to go and be by Foxx's side. "I heard my husband ask you who you were. But for some reason, you haven't told him yet."

"That's because he was talking to the other gentlemen and I didn't want to interrupt."

"He's not here now, so tell us who you are?" I heard Mrs. Foxx get straight to the point. She wasn't into mincing words. She likes to get right down to business.

"My name is John Andrews, and this is my partner Sarah Wayne. We're Internal Affairs and we're investigating the shooting between our officers and your son. So, if you don't mind we would like to ask you a few questions?" He wondered aloud.

"Go ahead I'm listening," Foxx said.

"Could we at least come inside?" Mr. Andrews asked.

"No. Whatever you gotta say to me, say it out there. Now if you don't feel comfortable talking to me from there, then I suggest that you go and talk to someone else. I never did like cops, and I especially don't like them now that I witnessed them slaughter my only son in broad daylight. And what's even more disgusting is that y'all let him lie down on the ground for hours with a fucking sheet covering him like he was a dead dog. I betcha animal control would've picked up a dog sooner than you picked up my son's body."

"Yes, it was deplorable how you guys treated my son." Mrs. Foxx interjected.

"I'm sorry you feel this way. But you do understand that your son fired at a couple of my officers first?"

"Well, it seems like you already got the answers to your questions. So, tell me why you're really here?" Mrs. Foxx continued. She was a wise woman. She can recognize bullshit from miles away.

"We're trying to figure out if your son fired his gun at our officers because he knew he was wanted by the DEA?"

"I don't know anything about that," Foxx answered.

Foxx was also a wise man. He knew that if acknowledged that he knew Reggie was on the run from the federal government that he and Mrs. Foxx both could be arrested for aiding and abetting a fugitive. I believe that was why he spoke up and answered that question before Mrs. Foxx did. He's a very smart man.

"Well then, are you aware that your daughter, Naomi Foxx is wanted fugitive?" The detective asked. "Because we got a credible witness that says she's hiding around here somewhere. And you two knows where she is."

That slick mother fucker knew what he was doing. He wanted to get Foxx to admit that he knew Naomi was a fugitive so that if he caught them aiding and abetting her, then they would get arrested on the spot. And I know Naomi, she wouldn't let the FEDS hold her parents. She would turn herself in for them. And that's what they would wanted.

"We're not answering any more of your questions. So, don't come back here." Mrs. Foxx said, and then I heard the front door close shut. "Fucking bastards! They better not knock on my door again. If they do, I'm filing harassment charges on them." Mrs. Foxx shouted. The mood in here has turned upside down. What are we going to do now?

Not My Family
(NAOMI)

To hear how upset my mother was really made me angry. If I wasn't on the run, I would give those cops a piece of my mind. I got up and hugged my mother when she entered back in the kitchen. I couldn't believe it, she broke down in tears right before me, so I held her tight. "Stop crying, mama. It's gonna get better." I tried assuring her.

"Naomi baby, you heard what that man said. They're looking for you. So, you're gonna have to get out of here as soon as you get the chance. I swear, I won't be able to handle it if I see them lock you up in a cage. I wouldn't be able to survive out here knowing that they took you away from me," she sobbed.

"Stop crying mama; you're making me sad," I told her.

"I'm sorry baby. I can't help it because I love you so much and it would kill me inside if they arrest you."

"She's right Naomi. You guys need to get out of here and get out of here fast." My dad agreed.

"You know we can't leave until we get the money," Damian said.

"Yeah, I know. I'm gonna get George on the phone right now and ask him when would it be a good time to time to go over there. 'Cause, tomorrow is the fourth day." My dad mentioned.

"Yeah, do that. The sooner we get out of here the better." Damian replied.

Foxx took his cell phone and walked down the hall to the back of the apartment, with Damian in tow. I hope they come back with some good news.

While my dad and Damian went to the back of the apartment, my mother and I stayed in the kitchen. I made her a cup of hot tea because I knew that was the remedy to calm her down. "Are you feeling any better?" I asked her after she took a couple of sips from her coffee mug.

"Honey, I just want all of this to be over with. But you know what?"

"What?"

"You and your brother wouldn't be in this life if I would've pressured your dad to stop hustling a long time ago."

"Mom, I'm not gonna let you blame yourself. This is not your fault."

"You may not believe it, but my father was a big-time drug dealer. He was the one that put your father on the payroll. It was like a family business for us. Now, look at you and your brother. He's gone. And now you're sitting here looking for directions. I can't tell you how to get out of this, but I can tell you that I love you very much. And if it ever comes a time that I don't see you again, just know that I will always be in your heart."

"Mom don't talk like that. We are going to see each other again."

"Okay baby girl, I can take that. But until we see each other again, always trust your instinct. And never let anyone tell you that is raining outside while the sun is shining. You understand?"

"Yes, ma'am,"

"Good." She said and then she took another sip of her tea.

"So, what are you going to do with Damian?"

"What do you mean?"

"He loves you. I can see it all over his face. Every time you walk in the room his face lights up."

I smiled because my mother was one of those mothers that knew everything. "Does dad know?"

"What? That Damian is in love with you?"

"Yes,"

"Yes, he knows. So, you know they're gonna have a man-to-man talk before you guys leave tomorrow."

"I'm sure," I said, giving her a half smile.

"We taught you everything you know, so make us proud."

"I will, mama," I assured her and then I leaned my head over in her direction and kissed her on the cheek.

Making Final Plans

(DAMIAN)

Foxx and I couldn't get George on the phone so we called his nephew Keith, and he answered his cell phone. "What's good?" he asked Foxx.

Keith didn't know that Foxx and I had him on speaker, so I remained quiet and allowed Foxx to handle the specifics. "Hey Keith, this is Foxx. Have you talked to your uncle?"

"Nah, why?"

"Because that's who I normally talk to concerning our arrangement and I didn't want to violate the chain of command."

"Don't worry about that. You're good."

"Cool. Well, you know that tomorrow is the day. So, I'm trying to find out what would be a good time to come and see you."

"I don't think tomorrow is gon' work."

"Why not?"

"Because I ain't gon' be ready tomorrow."

"You're kidding, right?"

"Nah, bro, I ain't kidding. See something came up, so I had to push the delivery date back."

"Back to when?" Foxx wanted to know.

"I can't say right now," Keith said nonchalantly. He was acting like he only owed us chump change.

"Hey look, Keith, I'm gonna need you to come with a better answer than that. We've got a lot of shit going on over here, and we need our money." I blurted out.

"Who the fuck is that?"

"It's me, Damian. So, come with a better answer than man."

"Listen, I ain't gotta do shit! I just told you that I had to push the date back. Now if that's not a good enough answer for you then, that's your problem, not mines." Keith roared on the other end of the phone. He really had his chest pumped up. But I was going to be the nigga that show him that he doesn't run shit but his mouth.

"A'ight, I'll tell you what. Give me back all my shit and let's call it even." I added.

"I won't be able to do that either."

"Why not?" I spat. I was getting more and more irritated with this guy by the minute.

"Because it's already in the streets."

"You mean to tell me that you put all four of those bricks in the streets?"

"Yep, that's exactly what I am telling you."

"Well, round up all the money you got, and I'll be over there to pick it up as soon as the sun falls tomorrow," I instructed him, and then I pressed the END button. I didn't want to hear that nigga say another fucking word. I swear, if I were in front of him right now, I would've snapped his fucking neck.

"Look, Foxx, I know you didn't like where that conversation went, but that guy was very disrespectful. And he was playing too many games with us. I know, without a doubt that if we would've had that conversation with him face to face, I would've shot him on the spot."

"I agree with you on so many levels. But remember he's got our money and our product. So, when we see him tomorrow, let's keep that in mind until we get our shit back."

"A'ight. Then that's what it's gonna be." I said, and then we shook on it.

Foxx was an old G. He's been around the block a million times, which is why I listen to every word he tells me. I don't take anything he says for granted. He's a real soldier. He literally taught me everything I know.

"There's something else I want to talk to you about." He said.

"What's up?" I asked, trying to feel him out. Trying to navigate where he was going with this conversation.

"You know I trust you with my life, right?"

"Yes, sir."

"You also know that I've always treated you like you're my own son, right?"

"Yeah,"

"When you leave here with my daughter, I want you to promise me that you are going to take care of her to the best of your ability."

"Oh yeah, Foxx. You know I got that part handled. I won't let anything happen to her."

"You gotta promise me, Damian."

"I promise, Foxx. I promise to protect til my last breath."

"Do you promise to always be kind to her?"

"Oh, hell yeah. I would never raise my voice at her or cheat on her. I mean that from the bottom of my heart." I tried to assure him.

"All right, well I'm gonna hold you to those promises. Now make me proud til that day when I'm able to call you my son-in-law. Okay?"

"I gotcha," I replied.

I swear, I didn't see this conversation coming from Foxx. I mean, we just got off the phone with a nigga that owed us money, and now we're talking about me taking care of his daughter. Damn! What a way to bring both worlds together.

It's About that Time

(NAOMI)

I was so glad that it was time to leave. Damian and I didn't have a lot to pack for our journey, so we were done within 20 minutes. My mother prepared a couple of meals and sealed them in Tupperware containers so that we could take them on the road with us.

It was my father's idea to let me drive him and Damian to Ivy Wild so that they could pick up whatever dope and money those guys had for them. It was also my father's idea that Damian and I put all of our things into the car so that as soon as we're done handling the money situation, we could drop him off at the corner of the apartment and then Damian and I could drive out of town. "Are you two ready?" My father asked us.

"As ready as I'll ever be," I said.

"I was ready before any of you." Damian followed.

"Well, let's go." My dad replied, and then he headed towards the front door.

My mother walked me to the door while Damian walked ahead of us. He did stop and kissed my mother before he made his exit. "Take care of my baby girl." She told him.

"I will. Don't you worry." Damian assured her.

"I want you to take care of yourself too." She added.

"I will mama." He concluded, and then he walked away from her.

"Please be careful out there. And make sure that you guys try to keep in touch. Even if you gotta reach out to me through my family in California. Consuela would be the one you contact. She still lives San Francisco. And she works for that homeless shelter down on 8th Street called The Sanctuary."

"Okay, mama. I will."

"Come closer so I can give you a big ole' kiss." She said and pulled my face towards hers. Without saying another word, she gave me the warmest kiss on my cheek.

"I love you so much, mama!"

"I know you do sweetie! And I'm gonna be praying for you two."

"Please do," I said, and then I took a couple of steps away from her. Before taking the third step, I looked back at her. "Don't forget to send me pictures of Reggie."

"I won't. Now get out of here before someone sees you." She whispered to me.

I waved at her and then I blew her one last kiss. "Come on let's go." I heard Reggie say from down the hall. It wasn't a yell. But it was loud enough for me to hear him, so I took off running into his direction. It's better to get away now then try to do it later.

When I walked in the parking garage with Reggie in tow, my dad Foxx was already in the car waiting for us. He waved for us to hurry up and get in the car with him. "Come on," Reggie said as he grabbed me by the hand. "Watch out for that camera on the left side." He continued as he pointed at the camera he wanted me to get by without anyone seeing me on it.

Taking it slowly, I followed in his footsteps. It took us about twelve footsteps to get by the camera. All we had to do was walk underneath it and just like that; we were home free. "It looks like you guys dodged the camera." My dad said after we climbed into the car.

"It looked that way to us too," I agreed.

"Good, now let's get out of this place before we run into someone else." My dad warned us.

I started up the ignition, and drove out of parking garage at the perfect speed, to prevent from drawing any unwanted attention. And when I exited the garage, I made sure that I slowed down so I could see what was around me. I had my dad and Damian scan the area around us too. We knew that the cops were looking for us now, so we couldn't take the chance of them seeing us and tailing us to a hot spot where we had to go to pick up our money. That would be the dumbest mistake I could make.

"Are we in the clear?" I asked them both.

"Yep, we're good." My dad said.

"We're good on this end too," Damian replied.

"All right. Well, let get our money."

We Came to Collect

(DAMIAN)

Foxx and I called George twice while we were in route to his nephew Keith's spot in Ivy Wild. Like before, he didn't answer our call. Once again, this infuriated me. Foxx started getting pissed off too. "What kind of game is this guy playing?" I asked Foxx.

"Don't worry about him. I'll deal with him later." Foxx told me.

It didn't take long for Naomi to drive us over to Keith's spot. As soon as we entered into the neighborhood, we saw a slew of crackheads swarming around the streets like bees on honey. It looked like an infestation.

"Oh my God! They look worse than the crackheads on 118th Street." Naomi criticized.

"You can say that again," I told her. She was right. These drug addicts were roaming around like they were zombies. "Pull over behind that black Honda," I instructed her.

"Is this where y'all are getting out?" She wanted to know.

"Yeah, so leave the car running, and we'll be right back." I continued.

"Foxx do you have your burner?" I asked Foxx.

"It's right here underneath my shirt."

A'ight, cool. Stay alert because I'm packing my heat underneath my shirt too."

"Let's do it." He replied and then we exited the car.

"Be careful you guys." I heard Naomi say before I closed the door.

"We got this, so keep the car running and pay attention to everything going on around you."

"Got it." I heard her say and then I closed the door.

I didn't say this to Foxx, but I was nervous as shit. I was totally out of my element. I had no idea how many niggas these dudes that nigga Keith ran with. For all I knew, this motherfucker could have a dozen soldiers in his crib. And all I had with me was Foxx. How lopsided was those odds? Now I could tell Foxx that we're in over our heads and that we need to regroup, but how would that sound? In his eyes, I would look like a lame ass dude with a pistol in my hands and not enough heart to use it. He could also think that I couldn't be trusted to protect Naomi. That would definitely crush me. And it would be hard for me to come back from that blow.

"Want me to knock?" I asked him.

"Yeah, go ahead." He insisted.

Bam! Bam! Bam!

"Who is it?" I heard a guy say on the other side of the door.

"It's Dee and Foxx," I answered him.

The other side of the door went radio silent. Foxx and I didn't hear a peep of noise. "Think they heard me?" I asked Foxx.

"Yeah, they heard you," Foxx assured me.

A couple seconds later, the front door opened. Behind the door was one of the niggas I noticed from the last time I was here. He was tall, but he wasn't that massive in size. "We're here to see Keith," Foxx spoke.

"Come on; he's in the back." The big homie said.

I walked in the house after Foxx did. And when the guy closed the front door behind me and locked it, that sound didn't make me feel easy. It was probably because the guy locked three separate locks, one after the other one. "Keep going down the hallway." He continued.

"We know where we're going." Foxx reminded him.

Finally, at the entryway of the room, Keith was in, both Foxx and I crossed over the threshold and Keith was in my sight. He was sitting on the end of one sofa, smoking on a big ass blunt. Standing around him were four other niggas. Two of them I remembered from the last time. The other two faces were new. "I thought I told y'all that I wasn't gonna have your money today." He said.

"Yes, you did say that, but we've got a lot of shit going on that needs to be taken care of, so we can't wait for another day," Foxx told him.

"Listen, old man; you might as well turn around and go back in the direction you came because you ain't getting shit from me," Keith said so boldly.

"Come on now Keith, let's not do this. Now, Dee and I came here in good faith, so we could make some money. We even went down on the price for you. And now you're telling us that you aren't gonna pay us? That's fucked up."

"It's gonna be more fucked up if you and that nigga don't get out of my face," Keith shouted.

"Does your uncle know what you're doing to us?" Foxx pressed the issue.

Keith burst into laughter. "He was the one who told me to shit on y'all because y'all niggas were wanted by the Feds. Did a couple of cops stop by your crib yesterday looking for your daughter?" He shared.

I swear, hearing this dude tell me and Foxx that George was the one that set this whole thing up felt like a kick in the gut. If George was in my face right now, I would put a slug in his skull without blinking. It would bring me much pleasure to see all of his blood draining from his head.

"Look, I'm getting tired of looking at you niggas. Get out before I sick my goons on you." Keith warned us.

"A'ight, we don't want no problems with you," Foxx said, and then he looked at me. "Let's move." He said. And immediately after he uttered those words, I knew what that meant. It meant that he was ready to go all out and kill every motherfucker in here. We turned our backs to them like we were getting ready to leave and in the blink of an eye we turned back around and started firing at every nigga in sight. I hit Keith first. Boom! Boom! Boom! Boom! Then I shot both of the niggas standing next to him. Boom! Boom! Boom! Foxx shot the dude that let us in the house twice, and then he shot at another dude that was standing off in the corner. But it was too late; the guy had already put a few slugs in Foxx. I watched him as he hit the floor. Boom! When I aimed my pistol at the nigga that shot Foxx, he made a run for it and fled on foot and ran out of the back door. His escape told me that he was either going to load up on more artillery or he was going to get reinforcements. Either way, Foxx and I didn't need to be here when he came back. So, I grabbed Foxx off the floor and dragged him as fast as I could down that long ass hallway. "Hold on, Foxx. I'm gonna get you out of here." I told him as I unlocked the door and opened it.

The Final Sacrifice

(NAOMI)

Fear consumed me immediately when I saw Damian dragging my father from Keith and his boy's spot. I hopped out of the car and rushed to their side. "What happened?" I shouted after I grabbed ahold of my father and carried the left side of his body weight over my shoulder.

"Naomi, let's just get him in the car before somebody sees up," Damian said, his voice sounding panic-stricken.

"Daddy, just stay with us. We're gonna get you to the hospital." I assured my father as we carried him back to the car. Tears were pouring from my eyes.

Immediately after we approached the car, I opened the back door on the passenger side and helped Damian lay my father down carefully in the back seat. "I'm gonna ride in the backseat with him," I told Damian.

"All right, but make sure you maintain pressure over his wounds. He's already lost a lot of blood."

"Daddy, stay with me. We're gonna get you to the hospital. Okay." I kept talking to him.

"Where is the nearest hospital around her?" Damian was shouting in the front seat. I saw him race through a red light and through several stop signs. I knew that if the cops saw the way he was driving, then he'll pull us over for sure. But I didn't say anything. At this point, I could care less about getting pulled over by the cops and getting arrested. My father's life meant more to me than me sitting behind bars.

"Pull up to that car and ask them," I instructed him.

Listening to my direction, Damian pulled up next to a BMW with a white couple in it and asked them where the nearest emergency room was. They told him that the nearest one was eight miles away. "Oh my God! Isn't that like seven to eight minutes?" I pointed out.

"Don't worry; I'm gonna get us there." He said.

"Daddy, keep your eyes open for me please," I begged him.

"I love you, darling." I heard him say.

"I love you too daddy. So, you're gonna have to stay with me. I'm gonna need you to keep breathing."

"I want you to tell your mother how much I love her."

"No daddy, you're gonna tell her yourself." I continued to sob.

"When I see your brother, I'm gonna let him know how much you guys miss him."

"Daddy, I'm not listening to you. You're not gonna tell Reggie anything. You're gonna stay with me. So, I'm gonna need to you hold on just a little bit longer. Okay." I said, waiting for him to say something else to me. But he didn't. "Daddy, what are you doing? Say something. I know you hear me." I wouldn't let up. "Daddy, say something please." I began to beg him. But to no avail, he wouldn't respond, and that's when I knew that he was dead.

"No daddy, don't do this. We can fight this together." I sobbed loudly while I held my father in the back seat of the car.

"You know that we're gonna still have to take him to take him to the nearest hospital," Damian said calmly.

"And do what? He's dead Damian!" I continued to cry. Tears were falling from my eyes uncontrollably as I rocked my body back and forth.

"Well then, what do you suggest we do?" He asked me.

"We need to talk to my mama first. She'll know what to do."

"Yeah, a'ight. But let me make a quick stop to that grimy ass nigga George. He's gonna pay for what he did to Foxx. And we will settle the score." He said, and then he fell silent.

Got One More Person to See

(DAMIAN)

It was my idea not to call George in advance. We wanted to catch him off guard so he wouldn't have any time to make any phone calls. After I knocked on the back door of his diner, he opened it and smiled. "Hey you guys, what's up?" He greeted us in a cool and laid-back manner. This guy would normally be all jovial when all of us in his company, but tonight, he was antsy. I could see right through this mother fucker. And I could tell that he sensed it. "Where's Foxx?" He asked, trying his best to keep the mood upbeat after he closed the back door and locked it. Before either myself or Naomi answered him, he noticed all the blood that Naomi and I had on our shirts and hands. "Hey, what happened? Why are you guys bleeding?" He tried to sound concerned.

"Don't stand there like you don't know what's going on. You know what the fuck happened!" Naomi snarled at George. She was on the verge of tears. And that's when I lost my composure. I took my pistol from underneath my shirt and aimed it directly at George's face. "Nigga, you sent Foxx and me straight into an ambush! You knew those niggas were going to murder us! You muthafuckas had your plan mapped out. You thought by calling the cops and telling them where we were, that they were going to come and arrest us and you, in turn, would be able to keep the coke and the money. But when that didn't happen, y'all figured that y'all didn't have any other choice but to rob us for our money and our product and then put us in body bags if we objected. But there was one problem. You forgot to tell those niggas that you can't get rid of New York niggas that easy! Yeah, dawg, we're New York's Finest, and we don't play any games when it comes to family and money. So, this is for my father-in-law." I said, and then I pulled back on the Glock and aimed the gun back at him.

"Come on Dee, it ain't like that. I didn't have shit to do with any of that. Foxx was like a brother to me! We grew up together on the same block." George pleaded, holding both of his hands in the air.

"Shut the fuck up! You're a fucking liar!" Naomi shouted.

"Naomi, I'm not lying! I loved your father!" George continued to plead.

"Shut the fuck up! You piece of shit!" Naomi shouted again. "Damian, give me the gun." She instructed me and then she held her hand out towards me.

Without saying a word, I gave Naomi my gun. There was already a hollow-point bullet in the chamber, so when Naomi took the gun from me, she pointed it directly at George. "This is for Foxx!" She said and then she let off three rounds. Boom! Boom! Boom! All three bullets hit George in his stomach and chest. He collapsed on the floor.

After she lowered her hand, I took my gun back from her. "Come on, let's see if he got some money around here," I said while I shoved it back down into the waist of my pants.

Naomi didn't help me ransack George's place. She indicated that she was going back outside to the car, so she could be out there with Foxx. I saw the pain in her eyes, so I let her go. But I warned her to keep her eyes open just in case we get an unexpected visitor. "Call me if you see someone coming," I told her.

"A'ight." She said and then she left.

I started searching through George's stuff in the office of his restaurant. I found a couple of checks he wrote to food vendors but they were of no use to me, so I kept searching and ran across his safe. Thankfully, it was slightly open. It looked like he was putting money away in the safe when I knocked on the back door. "Let's see what we got in here," I said as I opened the door of the safe wider. "Come to Poppa!" I continued after I saw four stacks of one-hundred-dollar bills. All four stacks of bills were wrapped in ten thousand-dollar strips, so I knew I had forty thousand dollars in my hands. There was also a .357 revolver in the safe too. I grabbed it and stuffed it down into my front pants pocket. George had a life insurance policy inside the safe as well. According to the document, it was worth $300,000. And the beneficiary was his daughter. "I know she's gonna be happy when she cashes this thing in," I commented, and then I stuffed the paperwork in my other pants pocket. I could've tossed the policy back in the safe, but it had my fingerprints all over it, so it had to go with me.

When I realized that George had nothing else of value to me, I walked out of his office, and then I headed back out the back door, and I didn't look back. Upon getting back in the car, I glanced back at Naomi and watched her as she sat in the backseat patting Foxx's hair. "You ready?" I asked her.

She hesitated and then she said agreed by saying yes.

"I found forty grand in George's safe," I told her while I was driving away from George's restaurant. But she didn't respond. Instead, she continued to cry between sniffles. I wished I could do something to reassure her that everything was going to be okay. But, I knew I couldn't because she just lost her pops. It's just a matter of time before Naomi's mother find out what happened to Foxx. What am I going to do?

Time to Say Goodbye
(NAOMI)

I got Damian to call my mother because I knew that as soon as I heard her voice, I would break down and ball my eyes out. When he got her on the phone, he told her to bring all of her things and meet us in the parking garage. It only took her few minutes to gather her stuff and meet us in the garage. As soon as she opened the front passenger side door the interior light and when she looked in my direction and saw me holding my father's lifeless body in my arms, she covered her mouth with both of her hands as the tears started falling from her eyes. By this time, Damian had gotten out the car so he could help my mother with her bags. "What happened? Is he dead?" I heard her say, her words somewhat muffled.

"Mrs. Foxx, get in the car." Damian insisted as he stood alongside her.

She wouldn't move an inch. "Is he dead?" She asked me.

I nodded my head as the tears started falling down my face nonstop.

"What happened?" she continued to question Damian and me.

"George set us up. He ordered his nephew to kill Foxx." Damian answered.

"That bastard!" She shouted and then she started crying uncontrollably. Damian grabbed her and pulled her into his arms. "Mrs. Foxx, we gotta get out of here." Damian continued.

"Leave here and go where?" My mother asked us.

"Anywhere but here," Damian replied.

"What are we going to do with my husband?" She wanted to know as she balled her eyes out.

"We were going to take him to the emergency and drop him off so that the coroners could pick his body up," Damian explained to her.

"You're gonna take him to the hospital and just leave him there?" She wanted clarity.

"Yes, ma'am. I mean, what else are we going to do with him?" Damian asked her. He wanted direction from her as to how to handle this situation we're all in.

"I can't in good conscience leave my husband here and runoff. First, it was my son, and now it's my husband. Oh Lord, what are you doing to me?" My mother said as she looked to the sky. "Take him out of the car and leave him here with me." My mother continued while wiping the tears away from the cheek area of her face.

"Are you sure you want me to do that?" Damian asked my mother.

"Take him out of the car right now. And y'all go before the cops find out that y'all are here." My mother insisted.

I watched Damian as he opened the back door and grabbed ahold of Foxx. I sat there, feeling as though I was paralyzed. I swear, I couldn't move one inch. It felt like everyone around me was moving in slow motion. I wanted to scream to the top of my lungs, but I couldn't get up the nerve to do it.

Immediately after Damian laid my father down on the ground near the car, my mother got down on her knees and cradled my father's head in her hands like I had done. She really started sobbing then. "Foxx, what am I going to do without you. First, it was Reggie, and now it's you." She cried out loud.

Damian kneeled down and kissed my mother on her forehead. "Mrs. Foxx, Naomi and I gotta go."

"Take care of my baby." She said.

"Don't worry; I will." He told her and then he hopped back in the car.

"Damian, we don't need to drive this car. We gotta switch and take Foxx's car." I suggested. I mean, it was only right. He and I can't ride around in a car that has all of my father's blood soaked into the backseat. That wouldn't be a smart move at all.

A couple of seconds later, Damian agreed and instructed me to get out of the car. "Mama, we're gonna take Foxx's car and leave this one here." I finally spoke up.

"The keys are in my purse." She told me.

Damian grabbed my mother's purse and removed the keys from it. "Got 'em! Come on Naomi, let's go." He said.

I grabbed my things from the front seat, bent down, kissed my mother and then I told her I loved her.

"I love you too baby. Please be careful. And find a way to check in with me once a week." She told me.

"I will mama. Kiss Reggie and Foxx for me when you have their service."

"I will sweetheart!" She assured me and then she turned her attention back on my father.

I was filled up with every emotion I could think of. I was once again on the run after losing my brother and my father. I swear, I can't deal with another loss. My heart wouldn't be able to take it.

After Damian and I got into my father's car, he started up the ignition, and when he drove off, I looked out the back window and saw a little glimpse of my mother sitting on the ground of the parking garage. I knew she was balling her eyes out. And knowing that, killed me on the inside. But there's one thing that's gonna keep me moving forward, and that's knowing that my mother is a strong woman and that she's going to take care of my father and my brother. She was a soldier. And so was I.

I don't know exactly where Damian and I are going right now, but I do know that it's somewhere far from here.

SNEAK PEEK INTO "THE BLACK MARKET PART 1"
(IN STORES 11/28/2018)

THE BLACK MARKET

BY: *Kiki Swinson*

PROLOGUE

It was closing time for the pharmacy so after I handed our last customer his prescription I escorted him to the sliding glass doors and watched him exit the building. While the doors were closing, I was caught off guard when three Middle Eastern looking men appeared out of nowhere and walked into the pharmacy like they owned the place. They pushed their way by me like I wasn't standing there. "I'm sorry, but we're closed." I told them. But my words fell on death ears. I watched them as they headed to the back of the pharmacy where Mr. Sanjay Malik was packaging up two large orders of Vicodin and Percocet that he planned to get rid of after we closed tonight.

I wanted to yell to the back of the pharmacy to forewarn Mr. Sanjay, while the men headed in his direction but I was instantly distracted when my cellphone started vibrating inside of my pants pockets. Immediately after I pulled my cellphone from my pocket, I looked at it and noticed that it was my cousin Jillian calling me. I quickly accepted the call and turned my body to face the glass front exit doors. "Hello," I answered quietly, in a somewhat whisper.

"Is everything still good?" She asked me.

But before I could answer her, I saw a broad reflection standing behind me through the glass doors. Startled, at the sudden appearance, I turned around. "Oh my God! You just scared the shit out of me." I made mention while I muffled my cellphone against my chest.

"Who are you talking to?" The Middle-Eastern looking guy asked me.

"My cousin," I told him.

"Tell your cousin that you're gonna have to call her back." He instructed me.

I was confused as to why he wanted me to end my phone call. I wanted to fight him on it, but I didn't. Instead, I placed my cellphone back up to my ears and told Jill that I will have to call her back.

"But wait," I heard her reply right before I pressed the END button.

"Give it to me." He instructed me as he held out his left hand.

"Is there something wrong?" I questioned him. Asking me for my cellphone was a weird request.

"Just hand it to me." He demanded and snatched it from my hand. "Did you lock the door?" He wanted to know.

"Wait, what are you doing?" I heard Mr. Sanjay yell from his station in the back of the pharmacy. And then I heard a slew of medicine bottles and boxes fall to the floor. I turned my attention towards the back of the pharmacy. But I couldn't see anything. Mr. Sanjay's station was out of view from where I was standing.

Not knowing what was going on in the back of the pharmacy spooked me. As far as I knew, Mr. Sanjay was being harassed by a small band of men and so was I. "Look, I don't know what's going on back there and I really don't care," I started off. I needed this guy to know that I wanted no parts of him nor those other men in the back of the pharmacy. "So, if let me get my purse from the back, I will leave immediately after."

"You aren't going anywhere." He told me in an eerie tone and then he grabbed me by the collar of my sweater. Acting off mere instinct, I tried to hank my sweater back from him as I took a couple steps backwards, simultaneously jolting my body hard enough for this guy to release the grip he had on me. Immediately after, he released my shoulders, I turned my back towards him so I could make a run for it since I hadn't locked doors yet. But as the door slid open, I was stopped in my tracks by yet another human being. "I'm not too late, am I?" The guy asked.

MISTY

I had only been a pharmacy tech for a period of like two and a half months. The job was easy and my boss Mr. Sanjay Malik was a dream to work with. The 5'11, forty-plus, cocoa complexion, Middle Eastern man, was not only a nice guy, he was very generous with the bonuses he paid me and he would occasionally let me get off work early. We had a delivery service for senior citizens that wasn't mobile to get their meds, so Mr. Sanjay would have me deliver their things to them and once I completed the deliveries, he'd tell me take off work for the rest of the day, which I found awesome. But after three weeks into the deliveries, I noticed that Mr. Sanjay had me delivering meds to dark and questionable neighborhoods. I never said anything to him about because who was I? And what was I going to get out of questioning him? He owned this place, which meant that he could fire my ass on the spot. So, I left well enough alone and minded my own damn business.

Mr. Sanjay wasn't aware of this, but I'd take a few pills here and there for my cousin Jillian. Jillian got into a bad car accident over a year ago, and hasn't fully recovered from it. Her doctor cut off her prescription meds six months ago so I stepped in.

The first time I stole two pills of Percocet and two pills of Vicodin. The second time I stole three pills of Vicodin and four pills of Percocet from Mr. Sanjay's locker. Each time I stole from him, the amounts go bigger and bigger. To my surprise he hasn't figured out that I've been stealing from him. I hope it stays like this too.

As soon as I walked into the pharmacy, I noticed that there were only three customers waiting for their prescriptions. I said good morning to everyone waiting as I walked behind the counter, clocked in and went to work.

It didn't take long for Mr. Sanjay and I to get his customers out of the pharmacy. Fifteen minutes later, they were given their prescriptions and then they were gone. "We got any deliveries?" I asked him while I searched through our online re-fill requests.

"I think we have about six or maybe seven." He replied while he processed another prescription request.

Mr. Sanjay was a very handsome man. He resembled Janet Jackson's second estranged husband. Not only did they look like one another, there were the same height and build. Unlike Janet Jackson's estranged husband, Mr. Sanjay wasn't wealthy to my knowledge. He owned this little pharmacy off the city limits of Virginia Beach, near Pembroke Mall. I will say that he's doing well for himself, which brings me to the question, why wasn't he married? From time to time I'd jokingly tell him that I was going to set him up with one of my friends. And his response would always be, "Oh no, believe me I am fine. Women require too much."

Not too long after I started working here, he told me that his family was from Cairo, Egypt. And that they were middle class citizen. Education was a big deal in his country. And arranged marriages too. "Think I could get me a man over in Cairo?" I would tease him. And his answer was always the same, "You wouldn't want a husband from my country, because the men are very strict and the women they marry are discipline. The things you say and do here in the US wouldn't be tolerated where I'm from."

"Yeah, whatever, Mr. Sanjay!" I chuckled.

Working at Mr. Sanjay's pharmacy was fairly easy. Time would go by so fast. The first half of the day, it would be somewhat busy and after 2pm, the traffic would die down. This was when I'd take my lunch break. If I didn't bring in my lunch from home, I'd leave the pharmacy and walk over to the food court inside of Pembroke Mall. This day was one of those days. "I'm going to lunch Mr. Sanjay. Want anything from Pembroke Mall?" I asked him.

"No, I'm completely find. But thank you." He replied.

I walked over to the computer, clocked out and then I left the building. On my way out, I ran into Mr. Sanjay's brother, Amir Malik. We both said hello as we passed by one another.

I've always found it odd that why Amir would always stop by to see Mr. Sanjay during my lunch breaks. And if I was there when Amir walked into the pharmacy, Mr. Sanjay would send me on lunch break or even send me home for the rest of the day. Now, I'm not complaining, because I loved when he'd let me leave work early, but at the same time, there aren't any coincidences in this situation. Something wasn't right with that guy and I knew it.

On the other hand, Mr. Sanjay did tell me that Amir lived here in the states too. He also told me that he was married with three children. And just like Mr. Sanjay, Amir was also very handsome. For some odd reason, this guy never talked to me. He'd wave his hands when he'd come and go but that was it. Nothing more, nothing less. I never asked Mr. Sanjay how old his brother was because you could clearly see that Amir was younger. He was never flashy. He always wore a pair of casual pants and a regular button-down shirt. He had the look of a car salesman.

I grabbed some Chinese food from the food court in the mall and then I took a seat at one of the tables near one of the mall's exits. While I was eating, I got a call from my cousin Jillian Torrey. Her father and my mother were siblings. My uncle committed suicide when we were kids so she lived with her mother until she turned 18. From there she's been back and forth from having her own apartment to sleeping under our grandmother's roof. Jillian was a pretty, 26-year-old full-figured woman. She wasn't the brightest when it came to picking the men in her life, but she had a good heart and that's all that mattered to me. "Think you can bring me a couple of Percocets on your way home?" She didn't hesitate to ask.

"Come on down Jillian not today." I griped.

"You're acting like I'm asking you to bring me a pill bottle of 'em." Jillian protested. "And besides you know I don't ask you unless I really needed him."

I let out a long sigh and said, "I'm gonna only bring you two. And that's it."

"Thank you." Jillian said with excitement.

"Yeah whatever. You're such a spoiled brat." I told her.

"So, what are you doing?" She wanted to know.

"Sitting in the food court of Pembroke Mall, eating some Chinese food."

"What time do you get off today?"

"I think I'm going to leave about 7 o'clock since to Saturday."

"Has it been busy today?"

"Kinda sorta." I replied between each chew.

"So, what are you doing after work?"

"Trey and I might go to a movie."

"That sounds so boring."

"What do you want me to sit around all day like you and get high off prescription drugs?" I said sarcastically.

"Oh Misty, that was a low blow. You know I don't do this shit for fun. If I don't take those drugs I'm going to be in serious pain." She explained.

"Look, I know you need 'em, so I'm going to get off your back. But from time to time, you do ask me for more than you should have."

"That's because I be trying to make a few dollars here and there. Oh, and speaking of which, I got a business proposition for you."

"What is it now?"

"I got a homeboy that will pay top dollar for 20 to 25 pills of Vicodin."

"Jillian, are you freaking crazy! There's no way in hell that I'm going to be able to get that many peels at one time."

"He's paying $400. But I'm gonna have to get my cut off top which would be $100."

"Jillian, I'm not doing it."

"Come on Misty, stop being paranoid. You can do it." Jillian started whining.

"Do you want me to lose my job?"

"Of course not. But you're acting like you've never taken drugs from your job before."

"Look, I'm not doing it. Case close."

"Just think about it." Jillian pressed the issue. But I ignored her.

"Is grandma home?" I change the subject.

"She's in the laundry room folding clothes."

"Did she say she was cooking dinner?"

"Yeah, she said she was going to brown stew a pot roast."

"Save some for me." I told Jillian.

"You know I will."

"Still talking to Edmund?" I changed the subject again.

"I just got off the phone with his frugal ass!"

I chuckled. "What has he refused to pay for now?"

"I asked him to order me a pizza online and he told me that he ain't have any money."

"Doesn't he own and operate a janitorial business?"

"Yep."

"Then he shouldn't be broke." I said. "Look, just leave that fool alone. You give him too much pussy for him not to feed you."

"I know, right?!" She agreed. But I knew her like a book because as soon as we get off the phone with one another, she's gonna call that selfish ass nigga and act like her stomach isn't growling.

She and I talked for another ten minutes or so about her finding another job instead of sitting on her ass all day, crying about how much pain she's in. My grandmother let's her ride with that lame ass excuse but I know better. Then I figured that maybe my grandmother does know it but looks the other way because she enjoys Jillian's company and she doesn't want to be alone in that big house. Either way, Jillian has a free ride anyway you look at it. "Don't forget to put some of that pot roast aside." I reminded her.

"I won't." She said and right before I hung up, I heard her say, "Don't forget my meds either." My only response to that was a head shake.

What an Eye Opener

I headed back over to the pharmacy after I finished eating my lunch. Surprisingly, when I walked through the front door, there were about two people waiting for their prescriptions but Mr. Sanjay was nowhere around. I spoke to the customers as I passed them. "As anyone been helped?" I inquired.

"No. We've been standing here for about five minutes." An elderly white man said.

"He's right." Another white man spoke up. "I even peeped around the counter to see if anyone was there." He continued.

"Well, don't worry. I'll help you two gentlemen." I assured them as I walked around the counter.

I took both men's prescriptions and then I logged them into our system. Immediately after I did that, I searched the back-storage room where we kept our drugs and paraphernalia and to my surprise, Mr. Sanjay wasn't in there either. Alarmed, I walked to the bathroom and knocked on the door. "Mr. Sanjay, are you in there?" I asked. But he didn't answer. So, I knocked on the door again.

"Mr. Sanjay, are you in there?" I repeated and when I didn't get an answer, I slowly grabbed ahold of the doorknob and twisted it lightly, opening the door calmly. Once the door was open, it was plain to see that Mr. Sanjay wasn't in there.

The only other place I figured Mr. Sanjay could be was in the back of the building. So, after I closed the bathroom door, I headed in that direction. The door was slightly ajar so I pushed it open. "Mr. Sanjay, there you are." I said after I laid eyes on him shoving boxes in the trunk of his brother Amir's car. I could tell that he wasn't expecting to see me. He looked very nervous to say the least. While Amir continued to maneuver boxes that obviously came from the pharmacy, Mr. Sanjay walked towards me.

"Did you need something?" He asked me in a weird kind of way. The way he said it sounded like a mafia boss asking an innocent bystander who witnessed a murder, did he see something.

I was taken aback and I really didn't know what to say. But then it hit me. "We have two customers in the pharmacy that said they've been waiting for over ten minutes for someone to help them." I twisted the truth a little.

"Take care of them." Mr. Sanjay insisted.

"Okay, sure. No problem." I said and then I turned around and left him standing at the back door. I heard it close while I headed back to where the customers were. I smiled at them as soon as our eyes connected. "Sorry about that. He was in the back of the building signing for some deliveries." I lied.

"He may not want to do that the next time around, because instead of me and this other fella, waiting around, it might be some young kids robbing you guys for all of your prescription drugs." One of the white men said.

"I agree." The other man said.

"I will definitely make mention of that as soon as he gets back in here." I assured them.

Since Mr. Sanjay gave me the green light to process these gentlemen's prescriptions I ran straight over to the cabinet where the Percocet pills were stored. I knew I had a small window of opportunity to get these pills for Jillian so we can make a few extra dollars. Immediately after I grabbed the pill bottle I heard Mr. Sanjay open and close the backdoor of the pharmacy. My heart started racing at a fast paced while I struggled to open the plastic bottle. But to no avail, it didn't open for some crazy ass reason. I've never had a problem opening and closing pill bottle. "I'm so sorry you guys." I heard Mr. Sanjay say. So, I knew he was standing behind the counter near the cash register. Frozen like ice, I stood there not knowing whether to put the bottle of Percocet back in the storage cabinet or stick them in my pocket. I heard Mr. Sanjay's feet walking in my direction so I nearly panicked. "Misty, who are you working on first?" He asked me in a moderate tone.

Feeling like I was about to have an anxiety attack, I shoved the bottle of Percocet into my pants pocket. "Hey there you go," He said as soon as he saw me. "What are they waiting on?" He continued as he stood in front of me.

"Mr. Lewis is refilling Trexall. And Mr. Williams is getting another refill of Metformin." I told him while I placed my right hand over my pants pocket to prevent Mr. Sanjay from seeing the bulge.

"Get the Metformin and I'll get the Trexall." He instructed me.

"I'm on it," I said and walked away from him. I swear, I can't tell you how scare I was when Mr. Sanjay walked up on me. Do you know I would've shitted in my pants if he saw me with that bottle of Percocet in my hands? I couldn't lie and say that I had it because I was refilling one of those guy's prescriptions. No, that wouldn't have made any sense. I know one thing, I won't do it again. The only time I steal a few pills here and there is when I'm filling someone's order. Other than that, I'm gonna chill.

I don't know where the time went, but it came and gone right before my eyes. "You can leave now." Mr. Sanjay said.

I looked at my watch. "Are you sure? I mean, we'll be closed in fifteen minutes." I questioned him. But what I was really doing was trying to buy time so I could put the bottle of Percocet back. When I took a bathroom break an hour ago, I managed to take open it and take a few pills out of it. All I needed to do now was put the plastic bottle back into the storage cabinet. "Don't worry. I've got everything covered. There's a storm coming our way so get home safely." He insisted.

I sighed heavily. "Okay." I replied reluctantly. I mean, what other choice did I have? He was my boss. So, I wouldn't dare tell him that I just stole a few pills of Percocet from a brand-new bottle I grabbed from the storage cabinet and now I want to put the bottle back. If I did, I'd be asking this man to fire me on the spot.

"Don't forget to drive carefully." He reminded me.

"I will." I assured him as I grabbed my jacket and purse.

Sick to my stomach, I dreaded leaving the store. Why couldn't I be more careful? If I wouldn't have listened to Jillian, I wouldn't have this fucking big ass pill bottle in my pocket. I can see it now, after Mr. Sanjay goes through the inventory in the morning, he's going to look me in the face and ask me where was the missing Percocet bottle? And I'm going to have to tell him the truth because who else could've moved it. I'm was only employee. Or let's say that I did deny it, all he would have to do was look through his security camera. Now it wouldn't show me actually taking the meds because of the angle, but it may show the bulge of the bottle in my pants. Damn! I've really fucked up now.

Unfriendly Visitors

My stomach had a ton of knots churning all at once. I couldn't believe that I just walked out of the pharmacy with a whole bottle of Percocet. The bottle contained three hundred and fifty pills with a seal on it that had never been broken. Knowing the number of pills, I had on me was giving me an anxiety attack. After I got into my car, I sat there motionless. I thought of breaking into the pharmacy after Mr. Sanjay left but then I decided against it because of the high-tech security system he had installed inside and around the building. So, once again, I am fucked. Up the creek with no paddle is what my grandmother always says.

Twenty minutes passed by and I found myself still sitting in my car, which was parked across the street from the pharmacy. My body wouldn't move.

I couldn't get up the gumption to put the car key into the ignition. So, while I sat there in the same spot, I noticed Mr. Sanjay's brother Amir pulled back up to the pharmacy. But this time, he wasn't alone. I saw two guys with him. One was in the passenger seat while the other one sat behind the driver's seat. I watched them closely as Amir drove down the alleyway of the building and immediately after he parked his car, he and the guy in the backseat got out of the car together. When they closed the car doors, my heart took a nose dive into the pit of my stomach when I saw the guy from the backseat aimed a gun into Amir's back. "What the fuck?!" I uttered. But only I could hear me.

Not being able to answer my own question, I sat there in disbelief while I watched the guy from the passenger side follow Amir and the other guy to the back door of the pharmacy. "Damn! Something is really about to go down." I said to myself, at the same time trying to figure out why some guy would jam the barrel of a gun into Amir's back? What kind of business did they had going on?

Curiosity really got the best of me because without giving it too much thought, I got out of my car and crept back across the street. The sun was setting so I took advantage of the natural lighting outside. Meaning, it was light in some places and dim in others. The lighting of the front entryway of the pharmacy was dim so I tipped toed towards it. The moment I came within four feet of the building, I looked through the glass window and saw Mr. Sanjay being shoved around behind the counter. I could also see him explaining something to those guys Amir brought with him. Amir was nowhere in sight, so I wondered where he could be?

While I watched Mr. Sanjay being pushed around, I also saw him handing the two guys boxes of prescription drugs. I couldn't read at the labels because of my distance between them, but I know that whatever it was, those guys wanted it.

I stood there for a few minutes and when I thought that I had seen enough, I scurried back across the street, got into my car and then I left. In route to my grandmother's house, I called Jillian's cellphone. She answered on the seconds ring. "You gotta be calling me with some good news." She said.

"Girl, you ain't gonna believe me when I tell you what I just saw." I replied.

"What happened?" She asked me.

"Are you still at grandma's house?"

"Yeah,"

"Good. Stay right there. I'll see you in ten minutes." I told her and then disconnected our call.

Four seconds after I placed my cellphone inside the cupholder it started ringing again. Bothered by the shear sound of it, I snatched it out of the cupholder and answered it. "Hello," I roared.

"Hey, what's wrong with you?" The male voice asked. It was the same male voice that belonged to my ex-boyfriend Terrell Mason. Terrell used to be the love of my life. He was the hottest nigga in the city. Tall, dark and handsome was what everyone called him. I guess that shit went to his head because he turned into this arrogant and unapologetic nigga overnight. I put up with it because he was paying for me to go to school to get my pharmaceutical license with that party promoting business he owned and operated. But that all fell apart when he started cheated on me with bitches that was bold enough to come to knock on my front door looking for him all times of the night. The last straw for me was when he got one of those bitches pregnant. I gave his walking papers immediately.

"I'm irritated about something right now. So, I'm really not in the mood to talk." I told her.

"Does it have something to do with me?" He pressed the issue.

"No Terrell. Not everything I've got going on in my life has something to do with you." I pointed out.

"Can I see you later?"

"No."

"Well, when can I come over?"

"Now is not a good time." I told him.

"You keep brushing me off like I'm some random ass nigga that's trying to holla at you."

"Look Terrell, I don't have time for this right now. I'm gonna have to call you back later."

"You've been saying you're gonna call me back all week. And you still haven't done it."

"That's because I've got more pressing issues to deal with." I spat. This nigga was getting on my last fucking nerves. He's not relevant in my life at this moment. He had his time with me until he cheated. So whatever issues he has with me and my reasons why I won't return any of his calls is something that he's got to deal with because I've moved on.

"Is it another man?"

"No! What?! What are you talking about?" I roared. Having another man in my life was the furthest thing from my mind.

"Tell me the truth." Terrell insisted.

"Look, I gotta go." I replied and then I pressed the end button. And immediately after I ended his call, I sifted through my settings and blocked Terrell's phone number so he wouldn't call me back. I was over him and his cheating ass.

I knew I told Jillian that I'd see her in ten minutes, but I ended up getting there in less than six minutes. Jillian was on the front porch of our grandmother's house when I pulled up alongside of the curb. I don't think I parked my car good enough before Jillian made a be-line towards me.

"Misty, you got my ears itching." She commented after she got into my car.

"You're not going to believe what I just saw."

Jillian was an impatient person. She never likes to wait for anything. "I think Mr. Sanjay is working for some mafia type of guys."

"Why you say that?"

"Because right before I left the pharmacy, I saw Mr. Sanjay's brother Amir pull up with two other guys in his car. And when they got out of the car, one of the guys put a gun up to his back and pushed in to the back of the store while the other guy followed them. And then after they went through the back door, I peeped through the windows in the front part of the store and saw Mr. Sanjay being pushed around. I even saw him give those two guys boxes of prescription medication too."

"Yo' I can't believe that you're working for the mafia!" Jillian said with excitement.

I nudged her in her chest. "That's not funny."

"Yes, it is." She continued to chuckle.

"What if he's not? And what if those guys were robbing him?"

"You can call it a robbery all you want. But I believe that he's into some illegal shit." Jillian continued and then she said, "Speaking of illegal, were you able to get me a few pills?"

"Is that all you care about?" I was getting disgusted by the second.

"Whatcha' want me to dwell on that shit that happened back at your job?"

"Could you at least act like you're concerned." I replied sarcastically, simultaneously pulled the bottle of pills from my pants pocket and then I threw them at her.

Her eyes lit up like a Christmas tree. "You stole a whole fucking bottle of this shit?! She said with excitement.

I tried to cover her mouth with my hands, while I looked around my surrounding area. Jillian mushed my hands back towards me, "Quit it. No one can her me. It's fucking ghost town around here. Most of grandmother's neighbors and friends are in an old folks' home or dead." Jillian replied in a nonchalant manner as she ripped open the bottle of pills.

I slapped her on the thigh. "You really have no filter." I commented while I watched her into the pill bottle.

"I can't believe that I am holding this huge bottle of fucking Percocets. Can you even imagine how much money we're gonna make from them?"

"We're not selling all of those pills."

"Yes, the hell we are." Jillian protested and then she opened the car door and stepped out of it.

"Jillian, I'm not playing with you." I yelled as she slammed the car door. That didn't stop me from talking. I climbed out of the car behind her. "Hand 'em over Jillian." I yelled again after I slammed my car door shut.

Jillian totally ignored me and made her way into the house. Immediately after I walked over the threshold of the front entrance, I heard my grandmother's voice. "Where is Misty? I thought you said that she was outside?" I heard my grandmother say. Her voice was coming from the den area of her house which was in the back of the house and straight down shot from the front door.

"She's coming now." Jillian told her.

"Hey Nanna," I spoke as soon as I walked into the den. I walked over and kissed her on the cheek. My grandmother was the apple of my life.

She looked at me from head to toe while Jillian took a seat on the sofa across the room. I could tell that she was texting someone. "How's work?" My Nana asked me as I sat down on the sofa next to Jillian.

"Work's fine." I replied, simultaneously reaching for the pills bottle between her legs. Jillian used her left hand to push my right hand back.

"What is that you're trying to get from her?"

"My bottle of vitamins." I lied while still trying to get it from Jillian.

"That's an awfully big bottle. Why do you need so many?" My nana continued.

"That's the way it comes." I lied once more.

"I'll be right back." Jillian announced to my grandmother and I and then she hopped up from the sofa and raced down the hallway.

I wanted to get up and run behind her, but I was emotionally spent so I didn't have the energy.

"So, I hear that your mother is dating a new guy." My grandmother stated. My grandmother was a cute old lady. She kind of reminded me of the actress Mrs. Cecily Tyson. She was the nicest person in the world. The kind of woman that would take in a dozen of homeless people and feed them. She'll talk about how good the Lord was to her too. You can't get her to cook you some food without hearing about the Lord Jesus Christ. Those two went hand in hand.

"If that's what you want to call it." I replied nonchalantly. My mother's name was Kathreen Heiress and she was a fairly decent looking woman. Back in the day everyone called her Mrs. Diana Ross. She had the whole look. But after the relationship with my dad failed, she started drinking heavily and dated anyone that would give her the time of the day. Her favorite pastime is daily trips to the ABC store. My grandmother has tried to help her plenty of time by wanting to send her to an inhouse Alcohol treatment center, but my mother won't hear of it.

"Have you seen him?"

"A couple of days ago when I went by there to get my mail."

"What does he look like?" Her questions kept coming. I forgot to mention that even though she's very generous, she's also nosey.

"He's tall and slim. Looked like he played basketball in high school."

"Does he look like one of those city slicksters from the streets? You know that's all your mama deals with?" My grandmother commented.

"Maybe back in the day. He had on a uniform from bread company downtown. So, he's probably one of their delivery drivers." I told her. But in all honesty, my mother's new boyfriend doesn't work for no one's bread shop. I just told my grandmother something so she could leave me alone about that man. I could really care less. I had more pressing matters at hand and it sure wasn't that nigga my mother was fucking.

"How is your boss treating you down at the pharmacy?" She changed the subject.

"He's treating me good. I don't have any complaints." I lied. But I was about to shit in my pants from the mere thought of this guy. I was starting to contemplate about whether I should go back to work tomorrow. For all I know, those guys could've robbed him and killed him. I don't want to see his dead body on the floor in a pool of his own blood. I would've ever be able to recover from that. Now I've seen a few niggas on the block get their asses kicked, you know get a couple of bruises here or there and that was it. I guess I'm going to have to play this thing out by ear. There's no other way around it.

I sat there in the den area with my grandmother and boy could this lady talk. She asked me every question under the damn sun. "Did you know that fella that got arrested for selling all those drugs from his mother's house in Norfolk?" She started off.

"Grandma, there's a lot of people in Norfolk that's selling drugs." I responded casually. I mean, the statistics are being recorded every day.

"I'm sure you're right. But this fella, had set up a meth lab inside of his mother's garage. They took his mother to jail too. But I heard this morning that the cops let her go after realizing that she had no knowledge of what he was doing."

"Nah, I didn't hear about that." I told her. I wasn't really interested in the family affairs of that guy and his mother. I had bigger fish to fry and my cousin Jillian was one of them.

"Want something to eat? I cooked up a batch of salmon crochets. And I got a pot of turnup greens too."

"I'm really not hungry right now because I'll get a plate to go." I said, as I looked at the direction of the door that led out of the den. "Where did that granddaughter of yours go to?" I directed the question to my grandmother.

"It sounds like she went upstairs to her bedroom." She guessed.

I stood up from the sofa. "Let me see what she's doing." I insisted.

"How long do you plan on being here?" My grandmother wanted to know.

"Maybe another fifteen to twenty minutes." I replied as I exited the den area.

"Come and give me a kiss before you leave."

"I will." I assured her and then I disappeared.

I headed up the flight of stairs that lead to Jillian's bedroom but she wasn't there. So, I called her name. Got no answer though. I looked in the bathroom that was a few feet away from her bedroom and she wasn't either. So, I headed back downstairs.

"Did you see her?" My grandmother yelled from the den.

"No,"

"Check the front porch. She's always hanging out there."

"Thanks," I said and walked towards the front door.

Immediately after I opened the front door, I saw Jillian seating in the passenger side of a beat-up, smoked gray, 2-door Honda Accord. Irritated my Jillian's lack of respect for my wishes concerning the bottle of Percocets, I walked off the front porch and stormed towards the car. As soon as I got within a few feet of the vehicle, Jillian opened up the passenger side door and proceeded to get out. "Where's the bottle of Percocet?" I wanted to know. I gave her a hard stare.

"She gave it to me. And I sure appreciate it." The guys leaned over into the passenger seat so that I could get a glimpse of him.

I took my attention off the guy and looked Jillian head on. "Why the fuck did you do that?" I screamed. I was fucking livid.

"Stop yelling. You're embarrassing me." She tried to uttered quietly while she tried to close the passenger side door.

"No, fuck that! Give me back that bottle." I looked at the guy and demanded while I prevented Jillian from closing it.

"Listen, I don't know what the fuck y'all got going on, but I ain't doing shit. So, get the fuck away from my car before you make me do something really ugly."

Shocked by this guy's word, I realized that this guy was no push over and that he meant business so I released my grip on the door so that Jillian could close it shut. The moment after Jillian closed his door, he sped off down the block. I instantly turned my focus towards Jillian. "Can you tell me what the fuck just happened?" I hissed. I swear, I was about to lose my fucking mind. My adrenaline was pumping and my heart was racing at an uncontrollable speed.

"I just made you and I a shit load of money." Jillian spoke as she opened her hand revealing a wade of money.

"I don't care at that fucking money. Do you know I'm gonna get fired for stealing all of those pills? Mr. Sanjay may even call the cops on me too." I tried to explain.

Jillian grabbed my right hand and opened it. "Take this twenty-five hundred and tell me how it feels in the palm of your hands."

"It doesn't feel like anything Jillian. And it ain't gonna mean shit once Mr. Sanjay calls the cops on me." I expressed. I was so mad with Jillian that I wanted to smack the shit out of her.

"If what you told me really happened at the pharmacy tonight, Mr. Sanjay ain't gonna noticed that the bottle of Percocet missing." Jillian tried assuring me.

I stood there for a moment and then I said, "You better be right."

Jillian tried to embrace me but I pushed her back. "No don't touch me." I whined.

"Oh no, you're gonna let me hug you." She protested as she bear hugged me. "Now, come back in the house so you can get some of grandma's food."

On my way back into my grandmother's house I asked Jillian exactly how much did that guy pay for that whole bottle. "He gave me thirty-two hundred for 330 pills, so, I gave you $2,500 and I kept $750."

"What happened to the other 20?"

"I kept 'em." Jillian replied, giving me a look like I'd just asked her a peripheral question. I nudged her in the back making her take a couple of missteps as she walked over the grass in our grandmother's front yard.

"I bet you did." I commented.

Back inside my grandmother's house, I got me a plate of food so I could eat it later and then I said my goodbyes. I had a rough day and I figured the only way I'd be able to settle my nerves was to go home, take a nice, long, hot shower and get in my own bed so I could catch me a few ZZZZZ's.

Unfortunately for me, that didn't happen. I tossed and turned the entire night thinking about what Mr. Sanjay was going to say to me when I walk back into the pharmacy in the morning.

SNEAK PEEK INTO
"*Cheaper to Keep Her*
PART 1"
(IN STORES NOW)

CHEAPER TO KEEP HER
PART 1

Prologue

"**B**itch! You better open this fucking door!"

When I heard his voice, the banging and then the kicking on the door, my heart sank into the pit of my stomach. A hot flash came over my body at the sound of his deep, baritone voice. I could tell he was more than livid. I immediately started rushing through the luxury high-rise condominium I had been living in for the past six months. Duke owned it. It was time to put my Plan B into motion. Quick, fast and in a hurry.

"Damn, damn, shit!" I cursed as I gathered shit up. I didn't know how I had let myself get caught slipping. I planned to be the fuck out of dodge before Duke could get wind of my bad deeds. I had definitely not planned my escape correctly.

"Lynise!" Duke's voice boomed again with additional angry urgency. He started banging even harder and jiggling the doorknob. I was scared too death, but I wasn't shocked. I knew sooner or later he would come. After all the shit I had done to him, I would've come after my ass too.

"Lynise! Open this fucking door now!" Duke continued to bark from the other side of the door. He didn't sound like the man I had met and fell in love with. He damn sure didn't sound like he was about to shower me with cash and gifts like he used to. Not after all the shit I had done . . . or undone, I should say.

"Open the fucking door!" he screamed again.

I was shaking all over now. From the sound of his voice I could tell he wasn't fucking around.

"Shit!" I whispered as I slung my bag of money over my shoulder and thought about my escape. I whirled around aimlessly but soon realized that my Plan B didn't include Duke being at the front door of his fifth-floor condo. There was nowhere for me to go. It was only one way in and one way out and I damn sure wasn't jumping off the balcony. If it was the second floor, maybe I would've taken a chance but I wasn't trying to die.

"Fuck! Fuck! Fuck!" I cursed as I saw my time running out. Duke was a six-foot tall hunk of solid muscle. I knew I had no wins.

"Bitch! I'm about to take this fucking door down!" Duke screamed. This time I could hear him hitting the door hard. I couldn't tell if he was kicking the door or putting his shoulder into it. Although it was his condo, I had changed the locks to keep his ass out.

I spun around and around repeatedly, trying to get my thoughts together before the hinges gave in to his brute power. Hiding the money, I had stolen was paramount. My mind kept beating that thought in my head. I raced into the master bedroom and rushed into the walk-in closet. I began frantically snatching clothes off the hangers. I needed to use them to hide my bag of cash.

Wham!

"Oh my God!" I blurted out when I heard the front door slam open with a clang. I threw the bag onto the floor and covered it with piles of designer clothes. Things Duke and I had shopped for together when shit was good between us.

"Bitch, you thought I was playing with you?" Duke's powerful voice roared. "Didn't I tell you, you had to get the fuck out of my crib?"

He was up on me within seconds. I stood defenseless as he advanced on me so fast I didn't even have time to react. I threw my hands up, trying to shield myself from what I expected to come when he reached out for me. But I was too late. He grabbed me around my neck so hard and tight I could swear little pieces of my esophagus had crumbled.

"Duke, wait!" I said in a raspy voice as he squeezed my neck harder. I started scratching at his big hands trying to free myself so I could breathe.

"What bitch? I told you if you ever fucked with me you wouldn't like it!" he snarled. Tears immediately rushed down my face as I fought for air. "Ain't no use in crying now. You should've thought 'bout that shit a long time ago."

Duke finally released me with a shove. I went stumbling back and fell on my ass so hard it started throbbing. I tried to scramble up off the floor, but before I could get my bearings I felt his hands on me again. His strong hand was winding into my long hair.

"Ouch!" I wailed, bending my head to try to relieve some of the pressure he was putting on my head.

Duke yanked me up by my hair. Sharp, stabbing pains shot through my scalp.

"Owww!" I cried out as he wrung me around by my hair. I tried to put my small hands on top of his huge, animal hands, but it was no use. Hands I had once loved, I now despised and wished would just fall off.

"You thought it was all good right! You a fucking trifling ass bitch and I want you the fuck out of here!" Duke gritted. Then he lifted his free hand and slapped me across my face with all his might.

"Pl-pl-pl-please!" I begged him for mercy. But Duke hit me again.

I was crying hysterically. Partly from the pain of his abuse, but more so from our past. I would have never thought our relationship would come to this. It had been a long road and all I wanted to do was teach him a lesson when I did the shit I did. I never thought I would have been facing this type of torment.

"I want all your shit out of here, you scandalous bitch! And don't take nothing that I fucking bought!" Duke roared, then he hit me again. This time I felt blood trickle from my nose. My ears were still ringing from the previous blow to my head. He hit me again. I was sure he had knocked one of my teeth loose.

"Yo' Ak, get this bitch shit and throw it the fuck out," Duke called out to one of his boys. He never traveled anywhere alone. There were always two dudes with him at all times. The one I knew as Chris rushed into the closet and started scooping up my clothes and shoes.

"Wait!" I screamed, but it was for nothing.

"Shut the fuck up!" Duke screamed in response, slapping me again.

I could actually feel my eyes starting to swell. I finally gave up. My spirit was broken and my body was sore. I watched as Chris and another one of Duke's boys slid back the glass balcony doors and started tossing all my shit over. I doubled over crying. More and more shit went over and I was sure it was raining down on the beautifully manicured lawn below.

"Yeah . . . that's enough. Don't throw none of that jewelry or those furs outside. I got bitches I could give that shit to," Duke said maliciously. His words hurt. "A'ight bitch . . . ya time is up."

I shrunk back thinking he was going to hit me again. But he didn't. He grabbed me by the arm roughly. "Oww!" I cried out.

Duke was squeezing my arm so hard the pain was crazy. "Let's go," he said, pulling me towards the door.

"Nooooo!" I screamed and then I dropped my body weight down towards the floor so he couldn't pull me.

"Oh bitch, you getting the fuck outta here," Duke roared. He bent down, hoisted me over his shoulder and started carrying me kicking and screaming towards the door.

"You can't do this to me! You will regret this Duke Carrington!!" I hollered.

"Fuck you!" he spat in return, opening the condo door and tossing me out into the hallway like a piece of discarded trash. I can't even describe the feeling that came over me. It was a mixture of hurt, shame and embarrassment all rolled into one.

Duke slammed the door in my face and I yelled for him to listen to me. My cries fell on deaf ears. My shoulders slumped down in defeat. Duke had left me in the hallway with no shoes, a short nightgown and nothing but my belongings on the lawn outside. I didn't even have the key to my BMW X6.

"Aggghhh!" I grunted in anger and frustration as I raked my hands through my tangled hair. I vowed from that minute on that Duke Carrington would learn just what all men have been saying for years . . . *it's cheaper to keep her.*

As I limped down the hallway of the building, all of the memories of how I had gotten to this point came rushing back.

CHAPTER 1
MAGIC CITY

One Year Earlier.

I walked into the *Magic City* and was immediately disgusted by the crowd that was already hanging around my post.

Same shit, different day, I thought to myself. I had been working at the well known strip club for a minute and it seemed like each passing month, more and more thirsty ass niggas showed up to spend their hard earned money on a fantasy. I crinkled my face and looked at my watch just to make sure I had the right time. It was only eight-thirty in the evening and niggas were already starting to pack the club. I mean, damn, didn't they have wives at home giving them some ass. Maybe not, judging from how they came up in the *club* and made it rain almost every night.

I noticed a few of the regulars sitting around. Of course, the ones that were there early were the older, more broke niggas that wanted to take advantage of the specials. The ballers usually rolled in after midnight and when they did all the girls who worked at the *club* would put their best foot forward and try to get some of that baller dough.

I scanned the bar area and rolled my eyes as I headed for my post behind the bar. I wasn't no stripper chick. Bartending was my thing. I could mix the fuck out of a drink, but I wasn't about to shake my ass for dollars. I didn't know how the chicks up in the *Magic City* did it. Men touching them all over their bodies for as little as a single dollar bill. Hell naw! Not me. All of those different hands all over my body, I would be sick after that shit. Then all that ass shaking, pole hopping and these chicks may or may not make a single dime. Not me, I needed guaranteed money. Even though these thirsty ass dudes didn't tip bartenders like they used to, they still wanted to sit up in my face and try to spit game my way. I probably turned down sixty niggas a night. I had so many of them telling me how beautiful I was. Yeah, yeah, I've heard it all. One nigga even told me I looked like Jada Pinkett Smith. Well, a few people told me that. Maybe it's true, maybe not. I did know that I was official. I kept my shit together: hair, nails and clothes. Although money was definitely an issue, the package had to be presentable.

As a bartender, I had listened to every type of story about life there was, especially the same old story men told about their dry ass wives at home who didn't give up the pussy. Yada, yada, yada. All that said, bartending at the *club* paid the bills. At least until a better opportunity came along, bartending was my gig.

I switched my ass past the early bird hounds who were already surrounding the bar trying to be the first to get their seats at the stage. It was Thursday, which meant, their favorite stripper was about to grace them with her presence.

Diamond was all the rage at the *Magic City* and she was also my best friend and roommate. She had left for work before I did since she had to set up her look and her music. She was the club's Thursday night feature. A different stripper was featured each night of the week.

Needless to say, Thursdays were when the club was most packed. All the men loved Diamond. I mean, she was beautiful. She had a sweet baby face and the body of a video vixen.

I was almost to my post behind the bar when I felt a presence. I jumped.

"It's about damn time you showed the hell up!" I heard the voice and then felt somebody grab my arm.

"What the—" My statement was cut off. I was a bit thrown off.

"Lynise . . . I need a big favor," Diamond said in a pleading voice. Her words rushed out of her mouth like running water. She looked as if she had seen a damn ghost.

"Damn girl, you scared me grabbing on me like that," I huffed, looking at Diamond as if she was crazy. "What's the matter with you?" I asked confused.

"I need to borrow some cash quick before Neeko gets here. I ain't got the money to pay for my sets tonight," Diamond said, with urgency in her voice. She was rubbing her arms fanatically. The nervousness was written all over her face. I hated when she acted spooked and it had been happening more often lately. I sucked my teeth at her.

"Why you need to borrow money Diamond? Didn't you do a couple of sets last night? I saw niggas making it rain all around you," I said, frustrated. There was no reason Diamond didn't have any money when I was sure she had probably made over five hundred dollars just the night before.

"I know but I had to loan some to Brian," Diamond replied.

I threw my hands up in her face. I already knew she had given her no-good ass, wanna-be hustler boyfriend her money. I despised Diamond's boyfriend, Brian, but I tried to stay out of her business. He looked and acted like a buster if you asked me. However, Diamond was madly in love with his raggedy ass. He always had his hand out. I told her a million times it was supposed to be the other way around. Brian should've been taking care of her and trying to get her the hell up out of the *Magic City.* That's the way I saw it anyway. But there was no turning Diamond against the slouch.

"How the fuck you keep giving that nigga all your money?" I barked at her. "He is a grown ass, able bodied man! If he can't hustle up money or go get a damn job then you need to leave his ass! You a sucka for love or what?" I was fed up with Brian or better yet, I was fed up with Diamond falling for his shit. He was always at our apartment, eating up our food and never lifting a finger or putting a dime in the pot.

Diamond put her head down and wore a sad frown when I told her about herself and her man. I knew I had hurt her feelings and I was immediately sorry. I loved Diamond. She was my road dog. We had been through hell and back together. Neither one of us came from good homes and we had been down for each other for years. I just wanted her to make better decisions and be smarter with her money. I guess I should have been a little more sensitive. But I was too mad to be nice.

"Lynise, I wouldn't ask you if I didn't really need this," Diamond said somberly, shifting her weight from one foot to the other as if she had ants in her damn pants. I noticed she was fidgety as hell.

"Yo, this is the last time I'm loaning you money Diamond. We both struggling to pay rent and bills, remember?" I chastised her, taking my bag off my shoulder and placing it on a barstool so I could get my wallet. I dug into my purse and handed her a hundred dollars. That was enough for her to pay Neeko so she could do a few sets and make some money. That would lead to more sets. I knew she hated doing lap dances, but I was sure she would be doing some tonight to get some extra money. It was part of the *game*. And as much as we hated it, sometimes the *game* ruled us.

Diamond smiled and snatched the money from my hand. Then she threw her arms around my neck and hugged me. "Thanks girl, you're a lifesaver, that's why I love you," Diamond said, all of a sudden in a cheery mood.

"Just go knock them dead tonight bitch, 'cause we need to eat dammit," I said jokingly. Diamond smiled. She was so pretty when she smiled. I smiled back. I really loved my best friend. I watched as she trotted off to go get dressed for her sets. I shook my head as she finally disappeared down the steps to the Magic City's dressing rooms.

"That damn girl gon' drive my ass crazy," I mumbled.

I still didn't see how she thought this stripping shit was the best thing. The strippers at the *club* had to give Neeko, the club owner, twenty dollars for each set just to let them dance in his club. Then they had to pay the DJ twenty-five dollars for each set to play their theme music. Diamond told me on a good night she usually picked up around two hundred each set. To her, that made it worth it.

I couldn't help but think about the bad nights. To me, none of it was worth it. The idea of having hundreds, maybe thousands of strange hands all over my body freaked me out. It didn't seem to really bother Diamond. However, deep down inside I think she felt just like I did about stripping.

One night, I watched from behind the bar as Diamond did her set. She got on her back at the edge of the stage, opened her legs like a scissor and spread her pussy lips open for a bunch of dudes sitting in the front row. I think she was just expecting them to throw dollars at her like usual. But I watched in horror as an old ass man, who I knew had no teeth, got up and actually put his mouth right on Diamond's spread eagle pussy and started slurping on her flesh. She definitely wasn't expecting it. The shock on her face spoke volumes. Diamond slammed her legs closed, smashing the man's head and he immediately jumped up. The man was smiling and wiping his lips. I thought I would throw up. Diamond looked horrified as she scrambled to her feet. The crowd of men burst into cheers and money flew everywhere. Although I could tell Diamond was disgusted, she stayed up there and picked up every dollar.

That night, as we drove to our apartment, neither one of us said a word about the incident. Once we got inside, I heard Diamond crying in the bathroom as she took a scalding hot shower. That's when I knew I would never, ever, strip for anyone.

I was four hours into my shift and I still had only made sixty dollars in tips. Talk about a slow ass night. I looked at the little chump change and sucked my teeth. Then just when I thought my night couldn't get any worse, in walks Devin, my sorry ass ex. I acted like I didn't see his ass at first, but he wasn't hard to miss.

"Wassup, Nini? You ready to take me back?" Devin said with a big smile on his face as he slid onto a barstool where I was mixing a drink for another one of the Magic City's regulars. I sucked my teeth and rolled my eyes at him. I slid the drink to my customer and rolled my eyes at the one dollar tip the cheap son-of-a-bitch placed on the bar. Devin noticed my disgust at the measly tip and of course he couldn't leave well enough alone.

"See, if you was still with a nigga like me you wouldn't have to accept those penny ass tips," Devin said, flashing his perfect smile. Although I couldn't stand his ass for what he had done to me, he was still fine as hell.

"If you could keep your dick in your pants, maybe I would still be with you," I retorted, folding my arms across my chest.

"C'mon baby, you met me in a fucking strip club . . . did you really think I could control that,"

Devin said snidely. I swear I could've slapped the living shit out of him. All my thoughts of finding him fucking one of the white strippers in the club's champagne room came flooding back. The nerve of that muthafucka! While I was right outside at the bar working, he was fucking this bitch.

One of the other girls had come and told me I needed to go into the back and check things out. Initially, I was hesitant, but she insisted. When I found Devin and that bitch, I went off. I hit him in the head with a Heineken bottle and I tried to rip that bitch's hair extensions from her scalp. Neeko almost tossed my ass out in the street over that shit. My forgiveness was paying for a couple of broken mirrors and tables. From that day forward, I vowed never to fuck with none of the club's patrons. Devin had taught me a valuable lesson. If a nigga is in a strip club, he ain't gon' be faithful for shit.

"You're a fucking animal. Get the fuck out of my face," I spat in response to his snide comment. I turned my back to him and went about my work.

"A'ight, suit yourself. When you ready to get out the hood, holla at ya boy," he said. Then he slammed a fifty-dollar bill on the bar. As bad as I needed that fucking money, my pride wouldn't let me take it. I snatched it up, crumpled it into a ball and threw it at him.

"Don't ever leave no money on this fucking bar unless you're buying a drink!" I screamed in a pissed off state over the music. "I don't need or want shit you got, you fucking pencil dick asshole!" That asshole just laughed. But I was seething inside.

My anger was overcome by the sound of Diamond's theme music. I immediately forgot about that fucking idiot, Devin, and turned to see my girl do her thing.

Diamond looked stunning in her all-white corset and thong set. She had feathers in her hair and her make-up made her look like an angel. I watched her jump up on that pole with the skill of a gymnast. She twirled around it, letting her long, dancer's legs sway through the air artistically. Once she slid down to the floor, Diamond did a full split and with one pull of a trick string her corset flew off. The men in the crowd went crazy when Diamond's perfect C cup breasts flew free. She lifted one of her perky breasts and stuck her long tongue out and licked her own nipple. That was it. More cheers erupted from the crowd and once again, more money flew.

I couldn't front, the woman was damn good at what she did. She knew how to work her body and work the crowd. She continued her dance until she was completely naked. Then out the corner of my eye, I saw Brian walk into the club.

"Shit!" I grumbled.

Brian never came to the club. He knew what Diamond did for a living and had agreed to stay away. I was instantly on high alert when I saw him. He was looking around with a crazed look in his eyes.

"Awww shit," I whispered to myself. I saw Brian walking towards the stage. I started to make my way from behind the bar. Diamond was making her booty clap and a few of her regulars were slapping her butt cheeks and putting money in her ass crack.

Before I could make it to Brian's location or the stage, he had rushed to the edge of the stage. He grabbed one of the customers that had his hands on Diamond's ass and punched the man in his face. Screams erupted and the DJ started yelling on the microphone for security.

"Brian!" Diamond screeched when she noticed what was going on.

The crazy muthafucka was outnumbered. All the guys in the front were together. Brian had just punched their boy. It was only a matter of seconds before the entire group jumped him. They had him on the floor punching and kicking him. Bottles were flying, chairs were being turned over. Then other niggas in the club just started going in on each other. Sheer pandemonium broke out. What the fuck? Did they think this was a John Wayne fucking western or what?

The security guards were truly overwhelmed and they couldn't get a handle on all of the chaos. It wasn't until the DJ screamed that the police were on their way that everybody started to scatter. When the raucous group of guys jetted from the *club,* Brian was left in a bloody heap on the floor.

"Get him the fuck out of here!" Neeko screamed. Security came to hoist Brian's battered body off the floor.

Diamond ran to his side. "Brian! Please wake up!" she cried out. She grabbed his battered head and his bloody skull covered her breasts. It looked like something straight out of a horror movie.

"This your man? Well you can get the fuck outta here with him," Neeko boomed at Diamond. Security put both Diamond and Brian out. I rushed downstairs and grabbed Diamond's bag with her clothes. When I got outside I helped her get dressed. When the ambulance got there, they put Brian in the back and Diamond climbed in with him. I watched as it pulled off. I covered my eyes with my hands. I had to get my thoughts together.

Finally, I turned towards the club and stared at the glowing sign that was in the shape of a stiletto heel. I shook my head, knowing I had to go back inside to get my things and my money. It was like my feet were cemented to the ground. That was how much I didn't want to go back into the club. I was so tired of working there. The whole club scene was taking its toll on me physically and emotionally. I stood outside as if I was standing at the gates of hell, waiting for the Devil to eat me alive.

The building I stood outside, looking at with disdain, was the hell I wanted to escape. It was my albatross. There was always something and I was growing very weary of the entire scene. It took some time to get my feet to move, but I was able to walk through the club doors to collect my stuff. I walked slowly and deliberately as I headed back towards the bar. I could see the trail of Brian's blood from the stage leading to the exit doors. Neeko was clapping his hands and having people clean up the mess.

"It's back to business up in here! One dead monkey doesn't stop the show! We got ass to shake and pussy to show!" Neeko was calling out as he rallied the other strippers and his little crew to get the club back up and running.

I was disgusted with the whole scene. I was amazed at Neeko's lack of remorse or compassion. I rolled my eyes and bent down behind the bar to retrieve my money. It was my secret stash. Money, I skimmed from the drinks I sold all night. That was the only way I could survive these days. I hurriedly stashed the money in my shoe and stood up.

I watched Neeko in disgust. He was acting like nothing had happened. "And tell your friend she is fired!" Neeko yelled at me.

"Oh please, Neeko . . . without Diamond's ass, this fucking club ain't gon' bring in no money, so I don't know who you fronting for," I spat back at his greasy ass.

Neeko paused and thought to himself. He knew I was absolutely right. There wasn't no way he was going to take a chance and let Diamond go work at one of the other competing clubs in the Tidewater area.

"Yeah, I thought that would shut you up. You will see Diamond's ass right up in here tomorrow night, so stop the yip yapping," I said sarcastically.

Neeko started yelling at the other girls. He knew better than to say anything else to me. I gathered my shit.

"I have to find a way to get the fuck out of this shit," I told myself.

I meant every word too.

I needed a way out and it had to be sooner . . . than later.

CHAPTER 2
EXCUSE ME MISS

The next night, I showed up to work dragging my feet.

My body language and attitude showed that I didn't want to be at the *Magic City* and to top it off, I was tired as hell because of all the drama from the night before. Plus, Diamond came home early that morning from the hospital and kept me up most of the morning talking about what had happened to Brian. I tried to be nice but I had to finally let Diamond know that I couldn't give a fuck less what happened to Brian's no-good ass. Sometimes I couldn't understand why she loved that slouch, but I guess love is blind and evidently, stupid.

Diamond and I arrived at the club together. We had ridden in her little hoopty, a beat up Honda Civic. My car was once again in the damn shop. I was glad Diamond had decided to go back to the *club* after how Neeko had screamed at her. She needed to speak to Neeko to straighten out their little rift and I wanted to get an early start before any of the other bartenders got the jump on the first paying and tipping customers, so we came in together.

"Good luck talking to that ignorant nigga," I said to Diamond prior to us going in separate directions once we were inside the club.

"I know, right. I just gotta suck it up, Nini," Diamond commented. "Shit, we need the money. The landlord will be knocking on the first and you know ain't no grace period with his ass." She was right. I shook my head in agreement.

"Gimme a hug, girl, I need it," Diamond said to me as we stopped near a table at the midway point between Neeko's office and the bar. I smiled and hugged her for moral support.

"Be strong and stand your ground. He needs you just as much as you need him," I championed, giving Diamond a pep talk.

When we let go of each other, I went to walk away when I suddenly felt the heat of someone's touch on my arm. At first, I thought it was Diamond, but when I spun my head around I noticed it was a man grabbing me. There was a group of them sitting at one of the so-called *baller* tables. I curled my face into the nastiest frown. I didn't play any of those strip club muthfuckas touching me. I wasn't a fucking stripper and I intended on making that shit crystal clear.

"Get off me!" I barked, snatching my arm away without really even looking at the man. "Keep ya hands to yourself! I'm not one of these working girls up in here," I growled and started walking away.

"Damn, you are so beautiful, even with that frown on your face," the man said in a smooth baritone that was enough to make my insides feel mushy. His voice made me look at his face. *He was fine.* I could feel my face getting hot and knew I was starting to blush.

"Look, I'm not interested. I don't strip and I don't fuck with strip club dudes," I said dismissively. The man laughed like I had told him a real funny joke. That just disgusted me more. I still couldn't help but notice the one dimple in his left cheek and how masculine and sexy his face was. He immediately put me in the mind of Boris Kodjoe, the actor. I quickly shook off the feeling I was getting about the fine stranger and stalked off towards the bar before he could make me blush anymore.

"You can't go that far, Beautiful. I'll be here all night and I'm not giving up," he called after me. I secretly smiled but wouldn't dare let him see it. He had called me Beautiful. *Cute pick up line,* I thought to myself.

After about an hour behind the bar, I noticed that the club started getting really packed. It was Friday and all the hungry patrons had gotten paid and were ready to play. That worked for me. I just prayed they were drinking as much as they were buying a feel and lap dance. I was hoping and praying for a good night of tips. Like Diamond had reminded me, there were bills waiting for my ass at home.

Diamond had made up with Neeko and she was about to headline, even though it was Friday and it wasn't her night. Neeko was a scumbag, but he was a businessman. He had given her the stage, which was a smart business move. He knew who his moneymaker was up in the *club.* That's why I didn't know why he was fronting the night before. I shook my head and laughed internally. Only a fool or dumb businessman would fire a moneymaker such as Diamond.

I was mixing two Incredible Hulks for a husband and wife duo that always came to the *club* to spice up their sex life when Diamond came behind the bar. She was smiling and her face looked kind of weird. I gave her a weird expression in return, because she hardly ever came behind the bar and invaded my workspace.

"Don't you need to go get ready?" I asked her.

"Girl, I got time. Mix me up something sweet, but heavy," Diamond demanded, her voice lazy and heavy. If I didn't know any better I would've thought she was high or some shit. As soon as the thought came into my mind, I quickly dismissed it. I knew better. Diamond and I had made a pact a long time ago . . . drug free always.

I passed the husband and wife their mixture of Hennessy and Hpnotiq, and as I pulled my hand away, somebody touched it. I sucked my teeth when I saw that it was the same guy from earlier.

"Your skin is so soft," he said, once again flashing his one dimpled smile.

"You wouldn't know that if you would stop touching me. I told you earlier I don't like to be touched and I ain't interested in the game you're selling," I said flatly. Then I turned around so I could mix Diamond's drink. I brushed off my feeling about her possibly being high and chalked up her behavior to being tired from her hospital stay with Brian all night. I knew she probably needed the drink to ease her nerves and get herself mentally prepared for her set.

The stranger stayed there, as if he was waiting for me to finish Diamond's drink. I had to admit, he was persistent. Most niggas would have already called me a stuck-up bitch and left me alone by now.

"Girl, that nigga that is trying holler at you is fine as hell," Diamond commented, laughing afterwards. She made it very obvious that she was talking about him too.

"I don't care if he fine or not. He is up in a strip club looking for some quick ass," I replied. I made Diamond a Pink Lady with an extra shot of Jamaican 151 rum and passed it to her.

"Lynise, if he was looking for ass he sure wouldn't be sitting at the damn bar trying to talk to the bartender," Diamond retorted. "Plus, that nigga is definitely caking off. I'm sure you can see that from here." I heard the seriousness in Diamond's tone and saw it on her face. I thought about that statement and she was right. I looked back at the guy and he was staring straight at me, which brought back that hot feeling inside my stomach and chest. Diamond took her drink to the head so fast I was shocked. She was definitely acting a little different than her normal self.

"Anyway, if he was just looking for ass he would be after me . . . the one who shakes her naked ass shamelessly every night, not you, the goody two shoes who refuses to take her clothes off bartender," Diamond said sternly. "Now you better let that nigga holler at you before you find me fucking him and collecting all his paper." Then she turned and walked away. Her words had hit me like a ton of bricks. She had definitely put shit into perspective for me.

"Ok, your bodyguard is gone now, can I order a drink?" the man called to me. It was clear he was not the type to give up. Either that or he really thought I was *Beautiful* and he just wanted to get to know me. Reluctantly, I went over to him.

"What can I get you," I asked, arms folded and head cocked to the side. I continued displaying the same attitude because it had become so routine for me. It was a defense mechanism I had acquired over the years. I felt like I had to protect my feelings at all times. I wasn't down for no bullshit from none of these cats in Virginia. Between my fucked-up childhood and all the fucked-up cats I had been with over the years, I was not up for the dumb shit anymore.

"You can get me your number and a date . . . tomorrow," the man answered. I rolled my eyes again.

"No, what kind of *drink* do you want?" I hissed. This time he didn't press, he just started talking.

"Trust me, baby girl, I ain't your average cat," he responded immediately. "I see you got much attitude and I'm digging that. I'm glad to know you don't let these dirty strip club niggas hit on you just for tips. Believe me, I don't pick up chicks in strip clubs either. I don't even frequent these jive ass places. I'm only here for my worker's birthday. The young cats that work for me chose this place. You know how it is when you young and horny. Well, maybe you being a woman you don't know. But in any case, the young dudes chose this place. I can assure you this is the first and last time you will see me in here. I'm a businessman. I damn sure don't have to buy lap dances and fantasy pussy."

His tone was very serious and his attack direct. For some reason, something about the way he spoke struck me as sincere. A slight chill came over me. I believed every word that came out of his mouth and I liked what he was saying. Everything he had said impressed me. I softened my attitude a bit and I found myself involuntarily smiling. I felt kind of dreamy. I heard Diamond's voice playing in my ear as well. Everything she had said was true . . . if this man wanted quick ass, he wouldn't be pursuing me. Not to mention looking at this fine ass man, with his flawless, smooth caramel skin and neatly trimmed beard was making me want to get to know him better. I guess the huge diamond studs and iced out pinky ring also helped to sway my attitude.

He noticed me sizing him up. "I can see your brain working," he smoothly stated. "It ain't much to think about, Beautiful. I'm not the last two-bit nigga that hurt your feelings. I am a man. All I'm asking for is a chance to show you what I'm about."

I swallowed hard. That mushy feeling was definitely creeping back up on me. I was so digging the fact that he kept calling me Beautiful. I thought that was so respectful and gentleman-like. But I can't front. No matter how smooth and fine this stranger was, I was nervous to throw my hat back into the dating ring. I had been hurt one too many times.

"I'm Duke Carrington," the stranger introduced himself. "Since you seem to need a full background check, here is my card. Look me up on the internet and you will see just what I do." He paused with a quiet confidence. And he knew it. "Then give me a call so we can do something tomorrow. You don't look like you need a man, but

I damn sure wanna show you what a real man can do
. . . Beautiful."

Then he stood up from the bar. He placed two
fresh and crisp one hundred dollar bills down and
looked me directly in my eyes. "Make sure you call
me. Um . . . I didn't get your name," he said
quizzically. His eye contact was causing me to have
hot flashes.

"Lynise," I said, almost whispering. Shit, for
a few seconds, I forgot my own name. I was so in
awe of how smooth this cat was.

"I think I will keep calling you Beautiful, it
fits you so much better than Lynise," Duke the
stranger said. And with that, he walked away from
the bar.

And I watched every step he took.

CHAPTER 3
SUGAR DADDY

"Lynise Aaliyah Washington would you just pick up your damn cell phone and call the man already!" Diamond yelled at me.

We had just finished looking Duke up on the web. He had been right when he told me about himself. He was a well-known businessman in the Virginia Beach area. You name it, he was into it: real estate, landscaping, a few car washes, a couple of barbershops and beauty salons. Duke was a real entrepreneur. I read up on all his business ventures, but for some reason his style and swagger still made me feel that he was into something illegal. It was just a gut feeling I had.

"Give me that damn number then. I'll make a date with the nigga while Brian ass is laid up in the hospital useless as shit with broken ribs," Diamond said jokingly. At least, I think she was joking.

"Ok . . . ok . . . I'm gonna call him. He wanted to see me today and whatever we do has to be before I gotta be at the *club* for work," I told Diamond.

"Girl, fuck the club and Neeko! You 'bout to become the wife of a rich man and get us both up outta this hood," Diamond sang, laughing afterwards. She seemed in much better spirits and more like herself than she had been in a while. I guess that was because that bum ass Brian was out of her life for a minute.

After a few more minutes of going back and forth with Diamond, I finally picked up the phone and called Duke's number. When his sexy voice filtered through the phone I closed my eyes. Diamond was making all kinds of faces. I could feel her presence.

Duke and I spoke for a few minutes and he agreed to pick me up. I gave him the address of the Marriott that was a few miles away from my apartment. I wasn't ready to let his ass know where I lived just yet. Duke said he would pick me up at five o'clock. That only left me an hour and a half to get ready. When I was sure he was off the phone I turned to Diamond with a panicked look on my face.

"Ok Miss Bitch, I took your advice and called him, but now the nigga will be here in an hour. What the fuck am I gonna put on and do with my hair!" I yelled at my best friend. "That is not enough time to get something done and find something at the mall to wear."

"Girl, please. You know you got Indian in your family," Diamond joked, putting her hand up against her mouth mocking an Indian call. We both busted out laughing. But my expression turned serious. I wasn't one to panic, but I felt some mild anxiety coming on.

"Seriously Diamond, what am I gonna do with my hair and what will I wear with a man like that," I said, getting back to the issue at hand. "Not like he is one of these regular slouches from around here."

"Lynise, your hair is long and beautiful, put some water and gel in that shit and wear it curly," Diamond told me, her voice of reassurance. "See, now look at my shit, this is gotta-have-a-perm hair." She playfully patted her hair. "Not you. You got that curly girl shit and besides, I love when you take your hair down out of that ratty ass ponytail you wear all the time."

I looked in the mirror at my reflection. Maybe Diamond was right. A little water, some gel, some make up and one of her hot outfits and I'd be set for my date with the businessman.

It took me close to an hour to get ready. I chose a black, fitted pencil skirt, a white collared shirt, which I left unbuttoned all the way down to my cleavage, and a threw on a pair of red pumps. Not too dress down and not too dress up.

"How does this look?" I asked Diamond as I tugged at my skirt.

"Nini, you look so gorgeous. I haven't seen you dressed up in a minute," Diamond said, faking like she was wiping tears of joy from her eyes. Her ass was hilarious and I enjoyed when we got a chance to spend time together like this.

"Your ass is silly!" I exclaimed, laughing at her. Diamond had hooked up my make-up. The fire red lipstick was taking some getting used to. I usually wore tans and browns on my lips, because my complexion was a bit light for the red stuff. Diamond had succeeded once again in convincing me that the red lipstick was the right touch for my outfit. I took her advice, of course. If there was anybody I trusted with fashion sense, it was Diamond.

I paced the sidewalk outside the Marriot waiting on Duke. I hated that I was there before him. I wondered if that would make me look thirsty or desperate in his eye. Usually the man had to wait on the woman, but being that Duke was such a classy businessman, I didn't want to have him waiting.

I stopped walking for a minute because my feet were already killing me in the pumps Diamond had loaned me. *Cheap shoes were a bitch to wear.* Just as I folded my arms impatiently and shifted my body weight from one foot to the other, I noticed a beautiful sleek, silver Porsche 911 pulling into the hotel's driveway. My heart started hammering in my chest like a bass drum. The windows were darkly tinted so I wasn't even sure it was Duke, but my gut told me that it was him. Sure enough, he slowly rolled down the passenger side window and leaned down so he could see me. He was flashing that sexy ass smile again.

"Hey Beautiful, you ready to go?" Duke sang out. I smiled back. I had told myself I would let my guard all the way down with Duke. I wanted to give him a chance. I wanted to give myself a chance to be treated like a woman should be treated by a real man.

I climbed into the car and I immediately recognized the scent of my favorite men's cologne—

Platinum Chanel. I knew right then and there that if Duke played his cards right, he could have me, in every sense of the word.

"Beautiful you look so gorgeous tonight," Duke complimented me. I smiled and thanked him. "I have something real special planned for you. I know you work hard as hell at that little club, so a woman that works that hard also deserves to relax and play just as hard."

I was quiet. Sitting next to a man who was nothing but a gentleman, smelling good, in a hot ass whip and looking like real money. I was in heaven. I just needed a minute to take it all in.

Little old me, a girl from the hood that had been treated like shit since she was a kid. My mother and father were fucked up and I had knocked around Virginia living with various family members. I used to run away all the time and I thought hustling, street niggas were gonna save me from my life on the streets. I was wrong.

When I met Diamond, she was going through the same shit. We instantly hit it off and got an apartment together. She put me on to the *Magic City* and Neeko had tried to get me to strip. I just couldn't do that shit. So I started mixing drinks and became a full-time bartender.

Duke's car rode smoothly down the streets. I couldn't feel the bumps on the road. That told me the car was straight luxury. Duke was playing nice, easy going music and he was talking up a storm. I answered him if he asked me a question, but I didn't make much conversation. I was just taking it all in.

When we pulled up to the Virginia Beach Elegance Spa my mouth dropped open. This place was one of the top, high-class spas in our area and mostly rich people and celebrities frequented it.

"Oh, my goodness. I can't let you take me here, Duke," I gasped. I knew the place costs at least a stack for just a massage. I looked over at him with my eyes stretched wide.

"Nonsense," he replied. "The entire staff inside knows me. They're expecting you, Beautiful. Don't worry, when you get inside they will take your clothes and hang them up. I selected the super deluxe package for you and it includes everything they offer. And that is only the beginning of our day, baby."

I smiled.

"I told you when fuck with me and you would see what it was all about," he said as he climbed out of his car.

I started getting out, but he knocked on the window and put his hand up telling me to stop. I was confused and I shrunk back down into the seat looking at him like he was crazy. That's when I saw him coming around to my side of the car. He opened the door for me and stretched out his hand for me to take so he could help me get out.

"A real man opens doors for his woman," Duke said smoothly. I was screaming inside of my head. I swear Duke could've had my pussy right then and there with that shit.

When I emerged from the spa I felt like a new woman. The massage was relaxing and my face felt silky and smooth from the sugar scrub facial I had received. Duke was waiting front and center for me.

"You look gorgeous as ever, baby." he complimented, extending his arms for a hug. I walked up to him, embraced and squeezed him tightly. *I was had.* At that moment, I could've stayed in his arms all day and night.

"Thank you for everything. It was so nice and relaxing. I realize now why people with money always look so good. It's this kind of treatment that keeps them on point," I admitted, letting go of his broad shoulders so I could look into his face. I wasn't into fronting. Duke knew I was a struggling bartender and I wasn't trying to front like I was anything other.

"It doesn't stop there, baby. We are on our way to the next phase of the plan I have for you," he said.

Damn! There was more! I thought to myself. This man had already spent some serious cake on me. What else did he have in store? We got back in the car and pulled out of the spa's parking lot.

"There can't be more. You've done enough already," I said and I was serious.

"Beautiful, you need to eat, right? This place we're going to is swanky and nice. I'm a gentleman, I would never send you home hungry," Duke said laughing.

He whipped his ride down the highway and I kept looking at him out of the corner of my eyes. He was so damn fine. We pulled into a cozy little restaurant and went inside. They seemed to know him inside. Why wasn't I not surprised? The waitress had me a little vexed the way she kept saying his name with this seductive little voice. That immediately made me suspicious that maybe Duke had something going on with her in the past.

Why are you jealous? You are here with him and she is serving you, I thought to myself, putting my mind at ease.

"What's wrong? You look a little distant," Duke asked me.

"Nothing. I'm fine," I answered, trying my best to put my suspicious thoughts out of my head.

"Good, because I have one more thing planned for you before I take you home," he told me. I almost dropped my fork when he said he had yet another thing planned for me.

"You've done more than enough Duke," I said bashfully. Honestly, I didn't want him to stop. My indifference was getting the best of me. I didn't want him to think I was a sistah that wanted him to keep doing more and more for me.

"I already told you, I planned our day down to the hour," he replied. "It's all good, baby. Trust me." And I did just that. I finally put my defenses all the way down and made myself trust Mr. Duke Carrington, businessman.

After lunch, Duke drove me all the way to the mall near the Pentagon in northern Virginia. I was shocked yet again. I didn't shop at that mall. I wasn't modest. I couldn't afford to shop at that mall. The mall had high-end stores such as Burberry and Saks

Fifth Avenue. Diamond and I always talked about one day being able to shop at places like Saks Fifth Avenue and Neiman Marcus on the regular. I smirked to myself thinking about my fantasy of a personal shopper showing me dresses that cost a stack and better.

"This is the last phase of my plan for us, baby," Duke informed me. "I want you to go inside and get the prettiest dress and shoes you can find. I'm taking you to dinner tomorrow and you need the best of the best for the place we're going." I was giddy. I just wanted to throw my hands around his neck and kiss him all over his face. But I remained cool and collected as we both exited the car.

Once inside the mall, I tried to stay as calm as possible but I wanted to just run around and grab shit. We went into Saks and a lady immediately approached us.

"Mr. Carrington, you're back," the old white lady said to Duke. He smiled at her.

"Yes, Caroline. This is Lynise . . . will you help her find the perfect dress and shoes," Duke said to the lady. I watched their exchange. It was crazy that Duke had a personal shopper and he was a man . . . that was usually for women.

"Ah yes, the perfect dress and shoes," Caroline repeated, laughing.

What the fuck is so funny bitch? I retorted silently in my head. I didn't know why she was laughing and I started to feel like she was mocking me in some kind of way.

"Go ahead, Beautiful, let Caroline work her magic for you," Duke said and he took a seat on a leather chair in front of the fitting rooms.

Caroline went and got about sixty dresses for me to try on. There was every named designer you could think of. I had never put my ass in a *Nicole Miller, Alexander McQueen, Versace* or *Herve Leger* dress in my life. Caroline also brought out about thirty pairs of shoes, most of them were *Christian Louboutin*, the red bottoms I had heard Oprah Winfrey talk about and saw her wear on all of her shows.

"Damn! Beautiful, you look amazing in that shit," Duke exclaimed when I finally came out in a crimson *Herve Leger* bandage dress. He made me blush. I whirled around for him in the tight fitted dress that looked like somebody had poured me into it.

"That's the one, Beautiful . . . that is definitely the one," Duke said excitedly. That was enough for me. I went back into the fitting room and took it off. I gave it to Caroline and she and Duke rang up the dress and a pair of hot red bottoms. I came to the register just in time to see that he had paid $800 for the dress and $695 for the shoes. I felt a little nervous letting a man spend that kind of paper on me. I started thinking that Duke might expect something in return. I mean we were in a recession and this man was spending that kind of money on me. I couldn't lie to myself though, I was damn sure glad Diamond had convinced me to go out with him. Even if shit didn't work out for the long haul, this one date was well worth it.

"Here you go, baby," Duke said, handing me my bags. "All yours," he smiled.

"Oh, my goodness, Duke, I cannot thank you enough for such a wonderful first date," I said and gave him a hug and a kiss on his cheek. I released him just in time to see Caroline smirking. I rolled my eyes at the old white bag. I told myself that bitch was just jealous. Maybe she wanted Duke too, just like the fucking waitress did.

"So, you want me to drop you back at the Marriot or to where you live," Duke said in a snide manner as we pulled back around my neighborhood.

"Well . . . um . . . you can take me home. The reason I—" I started to explain, but Duke cut me off.

"Baby, it's all good. I was really happy when you didn't give me your address right away. That told me you were smarter than most of these chicks out here," Duke interjected. I felt a sense of relief that he understood. Then I told him my address.

Duke pulled up in front of my apartment complex and I prepared to leave the car. He leaned over and kissed me softly on my cheek. I almost fucking melted inside.

"I will see you tomorrow night when you put that dress on," he said in a low whisper. I wanted to tongue him down so badly. I swallowed the lump in my throat.

"Yes, I will see you tomorrow. Thank you again for a more than wonderful day," I said softly. Then I kissed him back, also on the cheek.

I exited the car and flew up the stairs to my apartment. I rushed inside and called out for Diamond. "Diamond! Dee, you here?" I hollered. I raced into her bedroom but it was empty. Then I looked at the cable box, it was nine o'clock. Diamond was probably at the club already, I reasoned. Then it dawned on me that I hadn't called

Neeko to let him know I was going to be late for fucking work.

"Shit!" I cursed myself and went to pick up my cell phone. I dialed Diamond's cell first. I wanted her to tell me if Neeko had asked for me or find out what kind of mood he was in. Diamond's phone went straight to voicemail. "She must be on the damn phone with that bastard Brian," I mumbled.

I clicked off and went to dial Diamond's number again. I flopped down on our raggedy couch and started to press the send button on my phone. Suddenly, I looked over at the Saks bag and said fuck it. I didn't bother to call Diamond again. I figured I would just see her when she got home. I was no longer worried about Neeko's ass. "I will just show up tomorrow if I feel like it. Neeko don't be paying a bitch anyway and those fucking tips suck nowadays," I told myself.

I picked up my Saks bag and put on my new shoes and strutted around my apartment feeling like a star.

"I might just be quitting that fucking job soon anyway, when I become Mrs. Duke Carrington," I said out loud, *smiling from ear to ear.*

CHEAPER TO KEEP HER SERIES

AVAILABLE NOW AT:
;KIKIMEDIA.NET